DOGWOLF

Alden R. Carter

D0980581

SCHOLASTIC INC.
New York Toronto London Auckland Sydney

ISBN 0-590-46742-5

12 11 10 9 8 7 6 5 4 3 2 1   7   6 7 8 9/9 0 1/0

Printed in the U.S.A.   01

For my children,
Brian and Siri:
In beauty
may they walk

ACKNOWLEDGMENTS

Many thanks to all who helped with *Dogwolf*, particularly my editor, Regina Griffin; her associate editor, Tonya Martin, and assistant, Kim Stitzel; my mother, Hilda Carter Fletcher; Pierrette Boily, curator of Le Musée de Saint-Boniface, Saint-Boniface, Manitoba; my brother-in-law, Dave Shadis; and my friends Richard Montgomery, Don Beyer, Dean Markwardt, Steve Sanders, and Don Halloran. As always, I owe the greatest debt to my wife, Carol.

This project was supported in part by a grant from the Wisconsin Arts Board with funds from the State of Wisconsin and the National Endowment for the Arts.

CHAPTER ONE

Beyond the trees the dogwolf howled, its cry like a dull knife hacking at the blanket of heat and smoke haze thrown over the afternoon. I snaked the hose across the brown grass to the far side of the house, opened the nozzle, and played the water across the shingles. I'd rigged the hose straight to the pump to get enough pressure to reach the roof peak, but after fifteen or twenty minutes I'd lose it. And then . . . Well, it wouldn't make a hell of a lot of difference anyway. If a big fire got going upwind, a couple of garden hoses weren't going to save us, and we'd have to run like hell to make it to the highway before the flames cut us off.

I twisted the nozzle shut and walked back along the hose checking for kinks. At the pump house, I opened the outside tap, took a long drink, and then let the cold water run over my head and down the back of my shirt. Beyond the trees the dogwolf howled. If that damned thing didn't shut up soon, I was going to take my .22 down to the end of the road and shoot the bastard right in his cage.

I sat in the shade of the pump house letting my shirt dry while I studied the western horizon for signs of a big fire in the federal forest. Nothing, just the gray cloud that had hung over the forest all summer from the fires smoldering in the undergrowth and the peat. My stepdad would be out there again today with his crew, putting out one flare-up after another. That's the problem with a peat fire: humans can't get at it. Not all of it. Only steady fall rains followed by heavy snows and a slow spring thaw can put out a peat fire.

Mom came out the back door and stood beside the willow, holding her long braid against the back of her head to let the sweat dry on her neck. She called my name, not loud like a white woman, but in that way Chippewa women have of letting a word carry softly over distance. I waved from the shadow of the pump house.

She trudged over and sat down with a tired sigh. "Any of that lemonade left?"

"No. Want some water?"

"Okay." I got up, filled a tin cup from the tap, and handed it to her. "Thanks," she said. "Hot work cooking in that kitchen."

"Why bother? We could have sandwiches."

"Chuck's got to have hot meals. He can't keep going on sandwiches."

I nodded. The summer was grinding Chuck down. It worried Mom and it worried me. Chuck's a good guy. Not my real dad, but a good guy. I

2

filled the cup again for her, and we sat gazing at the cloud of smoke over the forest.

"It's thicker today," she said. "Smells hotter, too."

"Maybe a little. It's hard to tell."

"Aunt Loretta told me that there's going to be another rain dance Sunday week. They're bringing in a Kiowa shaman to give it a try."

"Why a Kiowa? Can't they find a Chippewa shaman? One of those *midéwiwin* guys?"

"There hasn't been a real *midéwiwin* shaman around here since before I was born. Besides, I don't think Chippewa shamans ever worried much about rain; it almost always rained around here. Anyway, the tribal committee tried to get that Hopi who was on *60 Minutes*, but they couldn't sign him up, so they're bringing in this guy instead."

"Can't hurt, I guess."

She glanced at me, a slight smile twisting a corner of her mouth. "Hey, let's have a little faith there, Pete."

"Oh, come on. Since when did you believe any of that stuff?"

"This summer I'm willing to believe anything. And you're too young to be a cynic."

"I'm half white. That gives me the right."

"Bunk. And you're not half white. Your dad was half and I'm only a quarter, so that makes you three-eighths."

"That's if everyone was telling the truth over the last twenty generations or so. Not likely, so I figure it rounds off to half-and-half."

We'd been through this a dozen times before, but the howl of the dogwolf interrupted before she could continue the routine. She stared at the spot where the road disappeared into the trees on the way to old man Wilson's. "I guess Wilson's still gone," she said.

"I haven't seen him come by."

"I wish he'd get rid of that darned creature. It's unnatural to mix dog and wolf."

I snorted. "That ain't a wolfdog or a dogwolf or whatever anybody wants to call it. It's just a big, dumb, mistreated dog. All the stories about it being half wolf are a bunch of bull."

"Maybe," she said, "but I still don't like it." She glanced at the circle of sun outlined in the haze. "It's almost time to pick up the girls. Do you want to go or should I?"

"I've only got a learner's permit, remember? I'm supposed to have an adult along."

"That didn't stop you last week when you drove over to Jim Redwing's."

"Special circumstances. His car wouldn't start, and I went over to give him a jump with the pickup."

"You always find special circumstances when it comes to Jim Redwing."

I shrugged. "He's the best friend I've got, and

4

he'd do the same for me. Don't worry, he's got a new battery now."

"Since when did Jim Redwing ever have enough money to buy a new battery? And why should he? He's always got you for a sucker."

"It's not a new new battery, but it's pretty new. He traded a good-sized doe for it."

Mom winced. "Is he violating again? He's going to get some serious sitting time from the judge one of these days."

I shrugged again, something I'd been doing a lot lately. "Jim's being cool. He just shoots a deer when he needs a few dollars."

"Well, keep out of it. I can't afford the fine for any poaching."

"Sure."

"I mean it, Pete. With court costs, that fine's over a thousand dollars now. Besides, the tribe made a deal with the Natural Resources boys that we were going to start obeying the game laws. And enforcing them, too. If Jim makes fools of the committee, they'll come down on him hard."

"I know," I said. "I've told him."

We sat for another minute watching the dull cloud over the forest. At last, Mom stretched. "So, are you going to get the girls or am I?"

"Hey, you just told me not to get caught violating. What's the big difference if I — "

She kicked my leg with the side of her foot. "Stop being a pain. You can drive three miles on back roads. You've been doing it for a couple of years. Keep off the highway and out of the ditch, and no one will care. Get going. I've got to get a cake out of the oven." She pushed herself up and then paused, very serious. "And Pete, really. Take it easy around Jim. If Chuck finds out Jim's violating again, he'll call the warden. He's got to; Chuck's a government man and a good one. I like Jim, too, but you can't let him drag you down."

"I know," I said. "Don't worry."

I dropped the old pickup into second and ground up the dusty drive to the Sorensons' place. My six-year-old half sisters saw the truck, jumped off the swing set, and ran to the house for their "pack-backs." Mrs. Sorenson gave me a wave and followed with MaryBeth, who's a few months younger than Heidi and Christine and used to play at our house a couple of times a week until the fires started getting too close. I swung the pickup around so that it pointed downhill, shut off the engine, and leaned back to kill the five or ten minutes the girls would need to find all their stuff. The wait used to irk me, but I no longer cared. Maybe it was the heat or the smoke or the dull headache I'd had for weeks, but even irritation no longer seemed worth the effort. I closed my eyes, letting my mind wander through the forest of eighths, quarters, halves, and miscellaneous fractions that made up my life.

Until this summer, all those fractions never concerned me much. I had a missing half-blood father, a three-quarter-blood mother, her full-blood relatives, a white stepfather, and two three-eighth-Chippewa half sisters who hardly looked Indian at all. None of it ever made any difference to me. Mom's Swedish grandad and my half-French dad had given me enough white blood so that I could pass for just about anything, and I bounced happily between white and Indian worlds, never getting hassled in either.

I don't know why, but I do know when I started trying to figure out the sum of all those fractions. I was standing on the ridge at the bottom of our front forty on a hot June night, watching the glow of the fires flaring beneath the cloud over the forest. And suddenly I had a picture of one of those fires slithering through a dry bramble patch and catching hold of something that was not brambles but a pair of old khaki pants, empty except for white leg bones. I've never been through a sweat lodge ceremony or fasted for days to have a vision, but that picture was so real that I felt the heat and smelled the chalky ash of my father's bones burning in that hidden place where he'd gone to die. And when the picture went dark, snapped off like a TV tube blowing out, I found myself on my knees in the dry grass, breathing like I'd run a mile. About then the dogwolf howled, and I was more scared than I'd ever been in my life, because for a minute I didn't know who I was or what was howling somewhere in the darkness beyond the trees.

That night, I lay awake for a long time trying

to remember my father. I was not quite four when he disappeared, and all I have is this memory of a crippled-up little guy who watched a lot of TV, drank too much, and sometimes cried when he held me on his lap while Mom did the supper dishes. He wasn't always like that. Mom's got this picture of him out in Idaho. Dad's just started up a big Douglas fir, a yellow hard hat on his head, a heavy safety harness slung across his chest, and a topper's chain saw hanging from the thick belt around his narrow waist. He's grinning at the camera, and even though he's far away, you can see that it's a cocky grin: He's a topper, one of the few with the skill and the guts to do the most dangerous job in the woods. He's immortal — a half-Indian, half-white demigod with a chain saw.

A year or so ago, Jim's uncle, John Redwing, told me about watching Dad work in the big timber: "Hank only had to walk around a tree once to know all its bends and twists. Then he'd go up the trunk like a bobcat, the spikes on his boots tearing chunks out of the bark. Just below the crown, he'd set his harness without even taking a breather and fire up his chain saw on the first pull every time. He always kept the chain sharp as a razor, and the chips would just spit out of that saw when he cut the notch. Then he'd kick out, swing around to the back side, pause maybe three seconds to study the crown, and then start cutting the hinge. When that top started going, he didn't hug the trunk like most toppers. He'd stay right at the

8

cut, nipping the sides of the hinge as the top gained speed so that once it let go, it'd fall just where he wanted it to. And I swear he'd be standing on the ground grinning at us before the branches stopped shaking." John let out a long sigh, his eyes distant with the memory. "He was one hell of a topper, Pete. One hell of a man. Never forget that."

But all that part of him was gone before I can remember, crushed the day the crown of a big fir spun on him just when he'd cut nearly through to the notch. And that crown came down fast with just enough of the hinge holding for all that weight to swing clear around the trunk like a giant fist to break half the bones in Dad's body. He was eighty feet up, and it took them nearly two hours to get him down in a sling.

Years later, long after she'd married Chuck, Mom told me how she'd left me with Aunt Loretta and driven an old '62 pickup west through a night, a day, and on into a second night: "There's so much country out there. I just drove and drove and never seemed to get anywhere. After a while, I couldn't cry anymore, so I just let that country have me. I didn't think, I just drove. And finally, I was sitting in front of the hospital in Coeur d'Alene, and for a minute I couldn't even remember why I'd come.

"I sat beside Hank's bed through all the weeks until they finally told me that they'd done all they could for him and that I might as well take him home. John Redwing and I got him as comfortable as we could on an old mattress, and with me riding beside him and John at the wheel, we started home. Over all those hundreds of miles, your dad never complained. He just rode with his gaze fixed on that big sky, while all that lonely country rolled past.

"When we could, we'd stop for the night at one of the reservations, where some of the women would bring us a hot meal and a few of the men would gather around the pickup to talk with John or just to stand quietly near Hank. I remember how different they were from the white loggers who'd come by the hospital in Coeur d'Alene. Those white guys meant well, but they were all full of bunk with their kidding and their telling Hank how he'd be topping trees again before he knew it. You only had to look at him to know that he was never going to climb another tree. Those Lakota, Crow, and Cheyenne men saw, and they didn't try to tell him different. Instead, they'd just stand by him for a while in silence, grieving with him for what his life had been." She sighed. "Indian people know how to grieve; we've had a lot of practice."

I waited a long time before she went on. "Often the priest would come, but Hank would never want to talk to him. So after a few Hail Marys and an Our Father, the priest would go away. Then a little while later, the men would step back to let the tribal healer through. Sometimes a woman, some-times a man, but always old. And the healer would give Hank something to drink to ease the pain and

10

then make medicine over him. They helped him more than the priests, I think, even though your dad had been a good Catholic all his life. It was like the white part of him was fading away. All that time he rode in the back of the pickup without saying anything for maybe a hundred, maybe two hundred, miles, I think he was looking into the Indian part of himself for something that could give him the strength to stand the pain."

"Did he find it?" I asked.

"I don't know," she said. "But he never complained to me. Not then, not later." She sighed again, tired of talking, tired of reliving what had happened so long before. I didn't ask any more questions; I knew the rest of the story. Or as much of it as anyone did.

That old pickup wheezed across twelve hundred miles of mountains, plains, and forests until they reached Lake Superior and turned southeast to bring Dad the last few dozen miles home. In the trailer where we lived then, Dad sat in a chair in front of the TV through the long winter days, while Mom worked and I played at the sitter's. Finally, he couldn't stand being a cripple any longer. So one April day, with the snow all but gone and the first buds turning the trees green, he went off to die. It took the search parties nearly a week to find the pickup stuck in the mud far down an abandoned logging road. They went on looking for another week, but he could have dragged himself miles into the forest before he finally gave out or found the right place to die. Anyway, they never found his body, and I doubt anyone ever will, except maybe Old Man Fire, and he doesn't tell secrets.

Chuck was washing at the trough beside the pump house when we got home. Heidi and Christine plunged out of the truck and ran to throw their arms around his long legs. He hoisted them one in either arm. Christine grabbed a handful of his long, blond beard, and Heidi tried to grab the pipe clamped in his teeth. "You're supposed to stop smoking," she yelled. "The doctor said."

Chuck laughed. "Okay, okay. Now let Daddy finish washing."

"You gonna throw that dirty old thing away?"

"Tomorrow." He let them down.

"Promise?" Christine asked.

Chuck laid a deeply tanned hand on his milk-white chest. "With my fingers crossed." He winked at me. That satisfied them, and they ran off to find Mom. Chuck put down the pipe and ducked his head in the trough. I handed him a towel.

"Thanks." He toweled his hair and beard vigorously. Chuck's a big guy, six four or a little better, but the two months of fighting fire had burned away every spare ounce of fat on him until he was nothing but bone and ropy muscle.

"How'd it go?" I asked.

He polished his wire-rimmed glasses with a corner of the towel. "We're holding our own, I guess." He gazed at the cloud of smoke on the western horizon. "But one of these days we're going to get something we can't handle. A good wind from the wrong direction and that whole goddamn forest is going to explode." He got out a comb and slicked back his thinning hair.

"There's going to be another rain dance on the rez. They're bringing in a Kiowa shaman."

"I thought that Hopi was supposed to be the best."

"I guess he's booked up."

Chuck grunted. "Well, I wish him luck. Personally, I'd rather have a couple of air tankers and a half-dozen crews of Blackfeet."

"Our Chippewa can't cut it, huh?"

"Oh, they're okay, but the Blackfeet are the pros. Trouble is, half the damned West is on fire, and there aren't enough Blackfeet to go around. A bog fire in northern Wisconsin is pretty small stuff right now. So, we're going to have to make it on our own until we can get some heavy support or some heavy rain."

I hesitated, already knowing the answer. "Can I join one of the fire crews? At least for a few days."

He shook his head. "Uh-uh. You've got to be sixteen."

"I'll be sixteen in November, that's close enough."

"Pete, we've been through this before. We wouldn't even be hiring sixteen- and seventeen-year-olds if we weren't so damned shorthanded that regional gave us a waiver. Besides, I want you here.

13

If that fire breaks loose, I'm counting on you to get your mother and the kids out." He lifted a hand to stop my protest. "But tomorrow, you can start sitting more tower. Mac called in this morning to say that Phyllis isn't feeling so good. He asked if you could start taking every other day. I said I didn't think you'd mind."

"I'd rather be in the action. Why not put old man Wilson in the tower? It's closer to his place than ours."

"Pete, look. I can't put you on a crew this year. No way. It'd be my butt if they found out that I'd hired a fifteen-year-old. As far as Wilson goes, I wouldn't trust that old drunk to watch a dead candle. Now, I know sitting tower gets boring, but it's important work. If we're fifteen minutes late hitting a hot spot, we could lose the whole works. Right now, we've got a pretty good fire line, but one breach and we're going to be in some very serious trouble. Believe me." He pulled on a clean shirt over his pale chest.

"Next year, I'm going," I said. "If there isn't a fire here, I'll go find one."

He studied me while his big fingers worked the buttons. "I hear you. And I won't stop you. That'll be between you and your mother. Fair enough?"

I nodded. "Yeah, fair enough."

"Good." He leaned against the side of the trough, sucking on his empty pipe and staring at the smoke cloud over the forest. The dogwolf howled and he glanced irritably in the direction of Wilson's place. "Seen Wilson today?" I shook my head. "The old fool has really gone on a bender, I guess. Well, you'd better go down there after supper to see if that beast has enough food and water. Personally, I'd just as soon shoot it, but I'll be damned if I'll let it starve."

"Okay," I said.

Mom came out the back door and waved for us. "Good. Supper's on," Chuck said. Halfway to the house, he laid a big hand on my shoulder, something he does awkwardly and rarely. "On the fire-crew business, Pete. I know you're strong enough and tough enough. And if the fire was a few miles farther away, maybe I'd take a chance on bending the rules. But the way it is, I want you here. If the big one breaches our line, it'll move fast. With a good wind from the west, it could be here in a couple of hours. Maybe sooner."

The big one. Sometime in the weeks since May, people had started talking about it, as if a really big fire was bound to happen no matter what anyone could do. "Then you think a big fire really could break the line?"

He stared at the cloud of smoke over the forest. "Yes," he said softly. "And it'll be like the end of the world."

Chuck and I have never said a lot personal to each other, so I was surprised to hear myself say, "You take care over there, huh?"

He smiled. "Sure. I got shot at for sixteen months in 'Nam; I'm not going to let a lousy fire get me. Come on, food's getting cold."

I climbed over the old split-rail fence, paused long enough to load my .22, and then started across the field toward the woods. In a normal year, Chuck sells two, often three, crops of hay off the front forty, but this year the grass lay bent and brown in the heat — a carpet of tinder waiting for a spark. The front forty rolls up against the low ridge where I'd had my vision of Dad's burning bones. I paused at the crest to look across the wooded country toward the smoke hanging over the forest. In the southwest, a thin line of dark clouds hung just above the horizon. I studied them for signs of hope or trouble. God knows, we needed rain, but we feared lightning even more. No one slept anymore when the thunderstorms came through, tossing bolts like giant matches into the dry woods.

I started down the far side of the ridge, where the land falls off in a series of gentle swells across our back forty. For three generations before Chuck bought the place, boneheaded Scandinavian farmers grazed their cows on the front forty and tried to grow corn on the back forty. But this is lousy farming country, and they got more rocks than corn. Chuck was smarter; he planted red pine. They're head high now, and if they don't burn one of these days, he'll have a marketable crop before he retires.

I followed the deer trail that winds through the red pine into the maple and birch beyond our property line. Once in the hardwoods, I kept my ears open for the chatter of red squirrels, but the woods were hot and still with no sound of animals or birds. It struck me that I hadn't heard the dogwolf since before supper. Maybe Wilson had come home while we were eating. Better to stay out of sight until I was sure. Sober, he was harmless enough. Drunk, you couldn't tell. Jim Redwing swore that the old bastard once fired a shotgun into the trees while Jim was walking through the woods on his way home from our place: "I heard his dog barking, not the dogwolf, but that yappy spaniel bitch that got run over on the highway a couple of years ago. Then all of a sudden . . . *Ka-whoom!* And it's raining bird shot. That *windigo* son of a bitch didn't give a damn what was out there; he just shot at the sound. I tell you, I was one very quiet, very fast Indian getting the hell out of there."

Remembering Jim's story, I moved quietly to the edge of Wilson's clearing and stood in the shadows watching for some sign of life. The place was old, must have been old long before Wilson himself somehow landed there. The cabin sagged at the corners, and the roof of the long, low shed on the other side of the clearing had buckled many winters ago. Only the dogwolf's cage was new, a twelve-by-twelve pen of heavy chain-link fence and eight-foot galvanized posts. There was no sag about it, no indifferent workmanship; it was built to hold and to hold anything. It held the dogwolf, a dark form padding, head down, back and forth across the cage. I watched, almost able to hear its steady panting across the stillness between us. It paused, seemed to study the spot where I stood, then turned back to its steady patrol of the cage.

Wilson's old truck wasn't in the clearing, and no light shone in the cabin window. But the truck could be in a ditch somewhere and Wilson home but still too drunk to bother lighting his Coleman lamp or building a fire in his cooking stove. I lifted my rifle and studied the dirty window through the scope. No help; I was going to have to go see. I hung the rifle on a broken branch and stepped into the clearing. The dogwolf whirled to glare at me, its hackles up, but it didn't make a sound as I walked past its cage on the way to the cabin. I knocked cautiously, then louder, and finally tried the door. It was locked.

The shed was empty except for a litter of rusty tools, twisted scrap iron, and empty metal drums. In the corner nearest the pen, I found half of a fifty-pound bag of dog food and a rusty pail that looked like it might still hold water. I filled the bucket at the hand pump in the yard and carried it to the dogwolf's cage. Wilson himself didn't go inside very often, and the flies and the stench were bad. I hefted the bucket and poured the water into

18

the length of rain gutter that ran to the empty water trough inside the cage. The dogwolf watched me, never blinking, never moving. I filled the bucket a second time and poured it into the trough. But although it must have been parched, the dog-wolf didn't move to drink. A second gutter led to a trough for food, but I didn't bother with it. Instead, I swung the bag back and heaved it over the top of the fence. That forced the dogwolf to move. It jumped back into a corner as the bag hit, scattering pellets of dog food across the cage. "Eat hearty," I said.

I took a drink from the pump and squatted in the shadow of the shed, watching the dogwolf. After a couple of minutes, it bent its head, sniffed at one of the pellets, and then walked disdainfully to the farthest corner of the cage and lay down. I couldn't see its eyes, but I knew that they were still fixed on me. "You bastard," I said. "Go ahead and starve to death." I walked to the woods, took my rifle from the branch, and started home.

I don't own a dog, never really cared to, but I've been around a lot of them. The harmless ones bark like crazy, their feet up on a fence, their throats and bellies exposed, and their tails wagging even while they're trying to sound like they want to rip your guts out. Shout at them, give the fence a kick, and they'll back off, all whining apology. The mean ones charge a fence, snarling, salivating, and generally making fools out of themselves. They'll bounce off and do it again just to make sure you got the point. Those you ignore, unless you have a mind to grab a two-by-four and beat some respect into their thick heads. Dogs that are really dangerous don't make any noise at all. They come toward you slow, heads down, throats protected, and murder on their minds. If there's a fence between you, no problem. If not, get ready, because you've got trouble. But the dogwolf wasn't like any of them. It never seemed to forget the fence penning it in, so it never bothered to make any show of what it might do if it got at you. I'd been in the clearing maybe a half-dozen times in the three years since Wilson had gotten the dogwolf and caged it up in the chain-link pen. But I'd never heard it bark and only once heard it growl.

Jim and I were hunting partridge on a Saturday last fall, and we'd come into the clearing to ask old man Wilson for some water. He gestured at the hand pump and went back to splitting wood. I pumped while Jim washed and took a drink. He was doing the same for me, when suddenly he spun and stared at the dogwolf. "What's the matter?" I asked.

Jim didn't reply for a long moment. "Nothing," he said. "Just thought I heard a deer or something out in the woods." He started pumping again.

While I was drying my face and hands and pulling my shirt back on, Jim walked over to the dogwolf's cage. When he was maybe five feet from the fence, the dogwolf growled low. Jim stopped in his tracks, and the two of them stared at each other.

Wilson yelled from over by the woodpile: "Get away from there, boy. That animal don't like Indians."

I grinned at Wilson. "I didn't think it liked anybody."

"It don't, and it don't like Indians in particular. If you boys are done, why don't you get along home? I think I hear your mommies calling." He gave the chunk of maple on the chopping block an angry swat with his mall.

I shrugged. "Okay. Thanks for the water. Come on, Jim."

Jim took a step backward, turned, picked up his pump 12-gauge, and led the way into the woods without a word.

I stopped at the top of the ridge to look again at the sky. The setting sun shone red through the smoke lying on the country, its light chalking the dry trees and dying grass a dull rose. To the southwest, the rising line of clouds thickened against the last of the light, and my eye caught a twitch of lightning low on the far horizon. And I knew it was going to be a long night.

Much later I'd think back and remember how the skyfire came down on the first night I thought of opening the cage door and setting the dogwolf loose.

CHAPTER TWO

The first thunder woke me from restless, sweat-soaked dreams of things I couldn't name. I threw back the sheet and tried to rise, but the heat weighed me down and I lay listening to the thunder and the stillness between. The storm would be over the western edge of the forest, the clouds balled up tight, the electricity feeling for the high crowns of the pines. And when the thunderbird blinked or the tension between positive and negative ions grew too great, a bolt would lash out and a great tree would explode, its crown torn apart as the electricity corkscrewed down the trunk like a berserk, million-kilowatt snake.

Downstairs the phone rang, and I heard Chuck moving, his bad leg dragging because he hadn't gotten it loose yet. His "souvenir from 'Nam," he called it. I climbed out of bed and tiptoed to the landing to listen. "This is Hendrickson," he said into the phone. He listened. "How big?" He listened. "Okay, I'll be there in thirty minutes." He hung up, sighed, and moved toward the bedroom to dress.

I heard Mom's sleepy voice: "Is it bad, dear?"

"Not yet, but they're calling in all the crews. I should have stayed there."

"You've got to rest. You can't keep going like this forever."

"I know. I know. Go back to sleep. Somebody'll call if a big one gets going."

"But shouldn't the rain — "

"Yes, the rain will help. Damp down the undergrowth a little, anyway. Now go back to sleep, Jan. I'll be all right."

I knew he wouldn't take me with him, but I was too restless to try sleeping again. I padded down the stairs and through the kitchen to the back door. Outside, the stillness itched with electricity. Around the yard light, a cloud of moths whirled, the lovesick flapping of their wings the only sound against the distant roll of the thunder. A shadow swooped down, snared a moth, and disappeared into the dark. Brother Bat or Night Swallow, I couldn't tell.

Chuck came out the back door. "Hi," he said.

"Hi. I don't imagine you want me to ride along."

"You imagine right." He stood for a moment, watching the steady pulse of lightning on the western horizon. He tightened his lips and shook his head. "Well, I'll see you later. Watch yourself."

"You, too," I said.

He got into his Bronco, swung it around, and bounced down the drive. I waited until the night swallowed the last glimmer of his taillights, and then reached inside the porch to flip off the yard light. I sat in the dark waiting for the rain. Or maybe for the fire.

I jerked out of a doze with the howl of the dogwolf in my ears and the sound of the wind coming through the trees like the downdraft of wings a thousand miles wide. The rain roared out of the woods and across the field faster than fear, and I was only halfway to my feet when the wind slammed me back against the wall. The boards of the old house creaked and seemed to bow, and I heard Mom slap her window shut and knew she'd be running to the girls' room next. But instead of going to help her, I braced myself against the wall and turned my face into the rain. I felt a shudder through my feet, and thunder exploded all around me. The willow by our back door writhed in the lightning flash, its tendrils suddenly ablaze with blue fire. I tried to scream for Mom, tried to warn her that the willow was on fire, but a lightning bolt as thick as a tree trunk hit the ridge, the crash of the thunder stunning me so that I stood deaf and dumb as the lightning rebounded in a ball of fire that rose fifty feet in the air, hung for a heart-beat, and then came spinning down the ridge toward our farm. At the foot of the ridge, it bounced, seemed to hang in air considering, then twisted itself inside out to swallow its own darkness. For a long moment, I thought it was still coming at us, its fire hidden in the cocoon of dark. But it was gone, and the wind let me go.

24

I slumped against the wall, sucking in great gasps of damp air, as the last raindrops pattered the roof and the branches of the willow swished lazily in the breeze. Mom called from inside the porch, her voice worried but hardly panicky. I tried to reply, but couldn't get out more than a gurgle. I cleared my throat and managed to call, "I'm here."

She flipped on the porch light and opened the back door. "What on earth are you doing?" she asked.

I shrugged. "Getting some air, I guess."

She raised her eyebrows. "Looks to me more like you got a shower." She grinned. "Better hope none of the girls from school drop by about now. You ain't hiding a whole lot in those soaked pajama bottoms." I looked down and covered myself quickly. She laughed. "I'm your mother, remember. Ain't nothing I haven't seen about you. Go put on something dry, and I'll make us a cup of cocoa."

Sitting at the kitchen table drinking cocoa, she didn't seem upset by the storm. I hesitated. "That was a pretty bad one," I said.

"What?"

"The storm."

"I thought it was going to be worse when the wind first came up, but it didn't do much after that."

"Lightning hit the ridge," I said. "A big bolt."

"Really? I didn't hear anything that close. Sure you weren't dreaming?"

I stared into my cup, unwilling to meet her eyes.

"I guess it was just farther away than I thought."

"I don't think you're getting enough sleep. I hear you wandering around almost every night."

"It's the heat. . . . That and some other things."

"What things?"

I shrugged. "I don't know. . . . I've been thinking about Dad some. Where did he come from? What was he really like? What happened to him? Stuff like that."

She watched me a moment before speaking. "I've told you everything I know."

"It's been a long time. I'd like to hear it again."

She sighed. "Bedtime story?"

"Yeah, bedtime story."

"Okay, but it's going to be a quick one." She paused, swirling the last of the cocoa in her cup. "I guess it's funny, but I really don't know a lot about your dad's life before I met him. He came from somewhere north of Winnipeg. His mom died when he was little and his dad was kind of a drifter, so Hank got passed around among the relatives. He never talked much about those years. Not that I think they bothered him or anything; he wasn't the type to worry about the past. He quit school when he was sixteen or seventeen and started traveling with one of those contract tree-planting outfits. That's how he landed here the summer after I graduated from high school. I was working in the hotel café, and he started hanging around. God, he was handsome. Only a hair taller than me and not much heavier, either. But you could tell by the way he moved that he wasn't afraid of anybody or anything. It's hard to describe, but he was like a big cat — graceful and powerful at the same time. And more than a little vain, too.

"Anyway, he asked me to go dancing, and I said no, because all us reservation girls were told to stay clear of the tree-planting boys, who were just out for sex and would be long gone before a girl found out what she'd gotten herself into. But he kept asking, and he was hard to resist with his big grin and his black eyes full of laughter. So, I finally said yes, although I knew Aunt Loretta would have a fit when she found out. And, oh, could he dance. I never danced with anyone better. All the girls in the hall that night were watching him, and half the local guys wanted to kill him. But he won over the guys, too. He had that way about him; nobody could stay mad at him for very long."

"What kind of dancing was it?"

"Oh, just country and western dancing. And don't think we didn't know how to rock, too, but neither of us ever cared for it much." She paused, thinking. "I remember that he said something kind of funny to me when we sat down during a break. He said that the dances were okay, but not as good as the ones they had back home. I asked him what kind of dancing they did there, and he laughed kind of embarrassed. 'It's really old stuff,' he said. Dances that came down to us from way back.' I asked him if he meant Indian dances because we had those, too. He said, 'No, no, they're French.'

Then the music started again, and he pulled me up. 'Someday I'll take you there and show you.' "

"But he never did."

"No, he never did. But you've got to understand that we weren't together very long. We were only married five years, and he was gone a lot of that time." I nodded.

"Anyway, the crew finished the job and one day he was gone. I was sad, but I knew I'd survive. Then about a month later, he walks into the café, sits down, grins at me, and says, 'I'm back. Want to get hitched?' " She laughed. "He was always saying stuff like that. I think he said it to me the first time we went dancing. So I laughed at him and said, 'Heck, you've only kissed me a couple of times.' And he said, 'Yeah, but that was enough to tell me you're the one.' And, you know, I actually begin to think he's serious. So I said, 'Well, ask me again after you've spent a little more money on me.' " She laughed. "God, he was a character, that's for sure.

"Anyway, he got a job cutting pulp, and we dated through the winter. He kept asking me to marry him, and that spring I finally said yes. A couple of weeks later, we drove up to Washburn and got married at the courthouse. I was nineteen, he was twenty. We were as poor as church mice, living in a drafty little trailer with ratty old furniture and so few dishes that we ate right out of the frying pan sometimes. But, boy, did we have a time dancing on Saturday nights and . . . well, being in love."

She paused, studying the bottom of her cup. "That lasted a little over a year until he went out West with John Redwing to earn some big money working in the tall timber. That's when your dad learned how to be a topper. And it became the love of his life. Not that he still didn't love me. Or that he didn't love you when you came along that fall. But topping gave him something he'd always wanted: a chance to prove that he was as big as any man and bigger than most. He loved the skill, Pete. He loved the danger. And that's what killed him in the end; he couldn't live without it."

We sat in silence, listening to the night breeze rustling the curtains. At last she went on. "After the accident, he wasn't the Hank I'd known. Not any part of him, except that he was still gentle. I knew that he'd never adjust to being a cripple, and I think deep down we both knew that sooner or later he was going to go off and die as quietly as he could. And he did die, Pete. Don't get into some fantasy that he went off somewhere to heal." She watched me.

"I know," I said.

She nodded. "Anyway, after he died, I tried to get in touch with his father. I had the address of a relative up there — a great-aunt, I think — and I sent the letter in care of her. I never got a reply, and the next time I wrote, the letter came back with a note from the postmaster saying that the old lady had died and that no one knew where Hank's father was. For a year or two, I expected to hear from the old man, but maybe he was dead, too, by that time. After a while, I just had to stop thinking about what might have been, so that I could go on living for you and for myself."

She sighed. "I look back now and think: God, what kids we were. Kids when we got married. Kids when we became parents. Kids when he died and I became a widow." She looked at me, tears in her eyes. "I haven't done that bad a job, have I? And Chuck's a good man. He's been a good father to you, hasn't he?"

"Sure, Mom," I said. "You've both done fine. I just wonder about Dad sometimes. . . . It's gotten to be a real strange summer, that's all."

She reached over and patted my hand. "I know," she said. "We're all tired. Even the girls. Maybe we'll get some rain soon." She glanced at the clock. "God, it's almost three. We've got to get some sleep; you're supposed to be in the tower by seven." She stood and then paused. "Try not to brood too much, Pete. Every boy goes through a strange time like you're having. In the old days, parents used to send their boys into the woods for a summer."

"Yeah, I know. They were supposed to paint their faces black and starve themselves until they saw a vision and got a personal manito."

Mom smiled. "That was the excuse, anyway. Personally, I've always thought it was to get them out of the house before they drove their parents nuts."

"Nice shot, Mom. Is that what you want me to do?"

"God, no. Too many mosquitoes, and I need you around here. Just take it a day at a time and try not to worry so much."

"Am I supposed to take you as an example on the worrying part?"

She laughed. "You really are a pain sometimes. Do you know that?"

"I work at it."

"Well, don't work too hard at it, boy, or you're liable to get me dangerously stirred up. And if you've ever seen a Chippewa woman that riled, you're not going to want to see it again."

"I'll remember that."

The rain had dampened the heat, but I still couldn't sleep. A little after five, I gave up trying. I dressed, ate a quick breakfast, packed a lunch, and was out the door before Mom or the girls were awake. I crossed the field in the gray light, intent on finding the burned grass left by the lightning strike on the ridge. But in twenty minutes of walking back and forth along the ridge, I couldn't find a single charred blade. Perhaps the bolt had hit one of the boulders half hidden in the grass and gone directly to ground. Either that, or I was losing my mind. Since I was still one of the saner people I knew, I liked the first explanation better.

I sat on one of the boulders still warm from

yesterday's heat and looked out across the forty acres of brown grass between the ridge and the farm, the memory of that spinning ball of fire clear in my mind. Whatever had happened in the night, somehow we had to get the field cut before something set it ablaze. For a month, Chuck had been trying to find a couple of free days, but the fires kept him too busy. When I'd offered to do it alone, he'd shaken his head. "No, we'd better do it together. God help anybody alone on a tractor if a fire gets started."

"That's not likely," I said. "I don't smoke or anything."

"Yeah, but you could hit a rock with the sickle bar and throw a spark. Or some grass could kick up on the muffler. It wouldn't take much. The only safe way is to have somebody riding along to watch for trouble. Until I can get some time, we'll just keep it cut back fifty or sixty yards from the buildings." I nodded, not liking it, but it's his farm and he's the boss.

We still call it the farm, even though it hasn't been a real farm in twenty or thirty years. Chuck bought it when he decided to settle down after a long time kicking around the country. He was raised in Kansas City and joined the marines after a year at the University of Missouri. It was, he says, "the dumbest thing I ever did." He went to Vietnam in a marine rifle company and, although he's never talked to me about the war, Mom's told me enough so that I've got a pretty good idea just

32

how bad it was. He was two weeks short of finishing his tour when a Vietcong booby trap nearly took off his right leg. After he got out of the hospital and took his discharge, he went home to Kansas City, packed his stuff in an old car, and hit the road. Over the next fifteen years, he had a couple of dozen jobs. Sometimes when he's talkative, he'll tell about working in the oil fields in Alaska, or with a harvesting crew on the Great Plains, or on an ore boat on the Great Lakes. He's seen a lot, and I envy him because I've never seen much of anything. Someday, I keep telling myself.

Some of his jobs paid pretty well, and he had quite a bit saved when he got off an ore boat in Duluth, bought another old car, and decided to have a look around northern Wisconsin. His car broke down close to here, and in the three days it took the garage to get the parts, he decided he liked the country. So he bought this old farm with its collection of rundown buildings and eighty rocky acres. He cleaned the place up, planted the back forty with red pine, and went looking for a job.

Mom was working in the Forest Service office and gave Chuck the application forms. When he handed them in, he asked her out for a cup of coffee. She agreed and that was pretty much that. Mom had been widowed for four years and needed a husband, and Chuck had been alone almost forever and needed a wife. Probably it was more romantic than that — it's always hard to tell with them — but they're both practical people and they decided to try living together through a Wisconsin winter before doing anything drastic. So, one fall day, Chuck shows up at our trailer, Mom hands him a couple of suitcases, and we drive out to the farm. I was seven and about half the size I am now, which still isn't big, and this guy is the biggest human being I've ever seen. But he's nice to me, and I don't mind when we don't go back to the trailer. All the rest of our stuff gets brought over a pickup load at a time, and in the spring they get married.

That fall, we moved a hundred miles south to Stevens Point, where Chuck enrolled at the university. I liked it okay in "da Point," but I was happy when Chuck finished his associate's degree in a year and moved us back north, where he went to work for the Feds as a forestry technician. Heidi and Christine were born that same summer, and after that Mom and Chuck pretty much let me go my own way. Which isn't bad. They trust me, I like them. We get along.

I followed the path through the hardwoods, the first rays of the sun slanting through the leaves. It was going to be hotter than ever, as the sun steamed off the rain we'd had in the night. I hesitated where the path split, one branch curving northwest toward the fire tower and the other swinging away to the east toward old man Wilson's. I hadn't heard the dogwolf howl since the instant before the storm broke, and I was curious if the bastard had survived the night. I imagined lightning striking one of the steel posts of the cage, the charge flashing around the fence to levitate the dogwolf in a sizzling electrical field. An instant of howling, convulsing agony, and then, *boom*, a hundred pounds of splattered blood, fur, and flesh on the chain-link. We'd all sleep better.

I decided to go have a look. This time I didn't bother to move quietly, and the dogwolf was on his feet staring at me when I came into the clearing. Wilson's truck was still gone, and the place looked even lonelier than the day before. I glanced into the cage. The water in the trough was down some, but as far as I could tell, the dogwolf hadn't eaten a single pellet of the dog food. I gave him the finger, crossed to Wilson's door, hammered on it hard, got no reply, and said to hell with them both.

I made it to the tower in good time and climbed the long steel ladder to the landing just below the ten-by-ten shack. I paused to catch my breath and then unlocked the trapdoor. A gust of hot, stale air greeted me. I clambered through and opened the windows before reaching for the power switch on the radio. There was a burst of static, and I heard far-off voices as the other towers started checking in. In all, there are nearly twenty towers ringing the forest. They're old and rarely manned except in really bad times, but they were all up on the radio today. I picked up the binoculars and scanned a full circle until I reached the smoke cloud above the smoldering peat bogs. There was a break

35

in the talk, and I thumbed my handset. "Crescent Lake, this is Tower One-One."

"Roger, this is Crescent Lake. You're loud and clear. How am I?"

"This is One-One. You're loud and clear."

"Roger. Who's One-One today?"

"Pete LaSavage."

"Hi, Pete. Steve Emanuel, here. Chuck says to tell you that he's not charcoal yet."

"Good to hear. Tell him to watch himself."

"Roger, I'll do that. Break. One-Seven, this is Crescent Lake. You up yet, Godmother?"

Stella Marston, the senior tower jockey and the only woman on the circuit, answered. "Been here half an hour waitin' for you boys to get done jabbering. You're loud and clear, Steve."

Steve laughed. "Roger, One-Seven. Break . . ."

While Steve finished checking in the other towers, I picked up the binoculars to give the country a slower scan. I caught a glimpse of the spotter plane circling lazily to the north. Maybe I'd learn to fly someday. I'd seen a movie once about the air tankers that drop water and flame retardants on the big fires in the West and Canada. The hero had been killed clearing a path to safety for a stranded gang of smoke jumpers who'd parachuted in to fight a wilderness fire. For months after, I'd dreamed about being a tanker pilot or a smoke jumper. But this summer, all my fantasies had withered in the heat. With the rain and the fall, I'd have to get my act together. Get a new girl, get

36

a life, start thinking about the future. The thought of Mona slipped in, but I pushed it away. No, that was all done with. If she hadn't found someone new by now, that was her tough luck.

"All stations, this is Crescent Lake. Here is the SitRep for July sixteenth." Steve launched into the daily situation report. "We got off easy last night. Lightning touched off three fires, but we've got two under control and should have the third one beaten down by noon. Coordinates follow . . ." I jotted down the numbers on the pad by the radio and then started plotting them on the map. "Now listen up for rules of the game, guys." Somebody keyed a mike and groaned; the rules were posted in every tower and we all knew them by heart. Steve was stern. "Knock it off. We're getting paid to do this, people." He started reading the rules.

I listened with half an ear as I finished plotting the fires on the chart. The biggest was in Chuck's sector, south and east of the smoldering fires in the peat bogs. I picked up the binoculars, found it, and studied the cloud of smoke. I'd seen worse. As long as we didn't get a wind, it shouldn't be too bad.

Steve finished reading the rules and began the weather forecast: hot, no wind, chance of thunderstorms late. The usual. He asked for questions, got none, and decided to repeat his usual cautions: "Now look, people, I hate to sound like a broken record, but you've been out there a long time and I don't want anybody getting careless. So stay on

37

this circuit and this circuit only. I don't care how boring it gets, stay off the fire-fighting circuit. Second, don't start thinking you're immune to lightning. We don't expect anything coming through until late, but the weather-guessers have been wrong before. Now the government's been generous enough to give you those nice grounded chairs for your protection. So, if something blows up, get on your hot seat and stay there until the storm's well past. And finally, people, if the big one gets going, don't anybody start thinking about being a hero. Tell me when you need to get out and then get out fast. Any questions?"

"Uh, Steve, this is One-Four. I had to take a leak and kind of missed the last five or ten minutes. Could you say again? Over."

There were a couple of hoots of laughter from other stations. Steve groaned. "One-Seven, can you give me any hints on how to deal with this crew?"

The godmother keyed her mike. "That's a negative, Crescent Lake. Not until you put missiles on that spotter plane."

"Not a bad idea. Okay, people, fun's over. Everybody give 'er a good scan and stay awake. Crescent Lake, Out."

The static hissed, and I was alone. The dogwolf's howl drifted up from the trees to the southeast. Well, the bastard hadn't lost his voice. Bad luck.

I got the log up to date. There was a note stuck between the pages from Mac: "Thanks, Pete. Know you've probably got better things to do, but I need some time with the wife." I turned over the sheet and wrote: "No problem. Tell her to send over some brownies when she's feeling better."

I drank a cup of coffee outside on the narrow deck that runs around the shack. I usually spent my days there with the radio receiver turned up and the handset within reach through the open window. I dragged my chair into the shade at the southwest corner of the deck, put my feet on the lower rail, and tilted the chair back against the shack. Every five or ten minutes, I took the binoculars from my lap and scanned the forest from the southwest to the north. Every twenty minutes or so — or when my backside got sore — I got up and made a slow circuit of the deck to check for signs of fire on the Chippewa reservation to the east or in the patchwork of forest and small farms to the south.

Steve's forecast had said no wind, but there's always a breeze above the trees, and by shifting my chair to keep in the shade, I stayed comfortable. For the first time in days, my dull headache receded, and I had to stir myself to keep from dozing. At ten, I answered Steve's radio check and was pouring another cup of coffee when I heard a shout from below. I went to the south side of the deck and looked over the side. Far below, Jim Redwing gave me a grin and a wave, leaned his rifle against a tree, and started climbing.

I got another cup and lifted the trapdoor for him. He got his breath back. "Whew, that damned climb is tough in this heat."

"It's nice out on the deck. Come on."

I took my chair and gave the forest a quick scan with the binoculars while Jim settled himself cross-legged against the rail. "Anything going on?" he asked.

"Not much. They put out a couple of small ones early, and it looks like they've got a handle on the only one that amounted to anything."

"Chuck's sector?"

"Yeah."

"I saw him in town a week or so ago. He's lost some weight."

"Yeah, it worries Mom. Me, too. You out trying to pop a deer?"

He gave me a look of offended honor. "Me? You know I don't do that stuff. I'm just trying to get some red squirrels. Heck, they're paying fifty cents a tail at the bait shop. Using them on spinners for the fishermen."

"Yeah, I know. But let's just suppose some clumsy deer just accidentally gets in the way?"

"Well, what can I do? I tell you, I've seen more tree-climbing deer this summer . . . I mean, it's weird. I'm drawing a bead on a squirrel and suddenly there's this big ol' buck just climbing right up there." He laughed.

I smiled. "Well, take it easy. There's some talk out, I think."

He was serious. "So I've heard. My uncle damned near had a heart attack when I brought that doe home. He said he's going to throw my 12-gauge down the well if I don't straighten up. So I'm carrying my .22 instead of old Buck Buster. And I really am looking for squirrels."

"I haven't seen many."

"I ain't seen shit, man. I think all the animals and birds beat it out of this country. Too damned dangerous around here with the drought and the fires."

"Getting that way," I said. "New boots?"

"Yeah. Uncle John picked them up for me down in Illinois. Like 'em?" He pulled up a leg of his jeans.

"Nice. That paw print on the sole should confuse Warden Bill."

"Yeah, I thought so. Give him the idea that there is one hell of a big lynx wandering around here. High-tops help the ankle some, that's the best part."

Jim's left ankle had been broken in a dozen places a couple of years ago when he'd dumped a motorcycle. It never healed right, and it kept him off the fire crews, even though he was a year over the minimum age. "Bothering you a lot?" I asked.

"Some. John wants me to have it looked at again. Maybe have another operation. I'm thinking about it."

"How is John?"

"Good. Truckin' a lot of pulp south. Gone three

or four days at a time now. When he's home, he spends half his time at AA meetings, so I don't see a lot of him."

"He still going with that woman he met there?"

"Nah, she started drinking again, so it looks like we're going to have to make it on our own."

"Tough luck."

"For her, I guess. Doesn't bother me much, except that we've got to eat our own cooking." He stretched. "I used to think it'd be nice to have a woman around. You know, to be kind of my step-mom, but I think I'm beyond that now."

I grinned. "Well, one of these days John might decide he'd rather have somebody to keep him warm at night than have you around getting him in trouble."

"Maybe. But I told him I'm going back to school in the fall, so I think he'll let me stick around for a couple of years yet."

"You serious about going back?"

"I guess. Beats peeling pulp. Besides, now that I've lost a year, we'll be in the same class and all I'll have to do is copy from you."

"No chance. They'll make you sit in the front. That's what they do with dropouts."

"No shit?"

I lowered the binoculars and looked at him. Hell, he actually believed me. "No, you'll be just like everybody else. Don't worry."

"You had me scared for a second. No way I'd go back if I had to sit in front. Hey, how's Mac's wife doing? I never would've quit school if I'd had more teachers like her."

"Not so good, I guess. I'm taking every other day now, so he can have more time with her."

"He looked worried the last time I saw him. Hardly said boo. Jeez, back when he ran the grocery store, you couldn't shut him up. Now he hardly says anything."

"Talked himself out, I guess."

"Could be," he said. He set down his coffee cup. "I've got to take a leak."

"Downwind is that way." I pointed over my shoulder.

I gave the forest another scan, wondering if I should tell him what I'd seen in the night. He'd probably accuse me of drinking bad hooch or chewing magic mushrooms, but I needed to talk to somebody about it. He came back, zipping his fly. "Pissing from fire towers. God, I love it. Maybe I'll forget about school and just travel around the country pissing from fire towers. Set a world record and become a TV celebrity."

"Dream on," I said.

He settled himself against the rail again. "Well, it was an idea."

"Get much rain over your way?"

"A little."

"How about thunder and lightning?"

"Not much. I think all the bad stuff slid to the south."

I took a breath. "I was out on the back steps

when the storm came through, and I thought I saw a bolt hit the ridge. Hit and bounce up in a ball of fire that came halfway down the ridge before it went out. Trouble is, I couldn't find a damned thing this morning. Not a single burned blade of grass."

Instead of laughing, he gazed at me before speaking. "Well, they say lightning can do funny things sometimes. Uncle John met a ranger in Montana who'd been hit by lightning, and all it did was blow a hole in the toe of his boot. John said he'd even seen the boot. But it's weird that you couldn't find any burned grass. Real weird." He shook his head and stared out across the dry country toward the gray cloud hanging over the forest.

I hesitated. "That's not all of it. Just before the lightning, the branches of the willow by our back door lit up with this blue flame. Then the bolt came down and the thunder just about knocked me over and the next time I looked at the willow, it was just like always. John ever tell about seeing anything like that?"

Jim didn't turn his head. "No, never did."

"Well, do you have any ideas?"

He was suddenly irritable. "Hell, you're the one who's good in school. I dropped out, remember. Don't ask me any of this shit." For a long moment, neither of us said anything, then he sighed. "Look, I don't know what's going on, and I don't think anybody else does, either. It's been too hot and too dry for too long. Everything's getting crazy. The *Windigo* is out there looking to eat us all."

Like every Chippewa kid, I'd heard the old folk-tales about the *Windigo* — the man-eating ice skeleton who stalked the winter woods in times of famine and whose name had become a word for craziness. "I think he'd melt in this heat." I laughed.

Jim didn't. "Yeah. Well, this time he's made of fire." He stood. "Better do your job before they can you. I'm going to get another cup of coffee."

He went inside, and I did a circuit of the deck to check for smoke in the other directions. The dogwolf's howl drifted up from the trees, and I heard Jim drop something and swear. When he came back out on the deck, I asked, "Come by way of Wilson's?"

"No. I don't like that damned dogwolf of his. Wilson doesn't either from what I can tell."

"Have you seen him?"

"About three nights in a row last week. He was tying on a good one. Throwing his money around pretty good, too. I drank my share of it."

"Where?"

"Eddy's, up off the Whetstone Lake road. Little place way back in. Ever been there?"

"Been by. What was Wilson doing way up there?"

"Getting drunk. What else?"

"Talk to him much?"

"Oh, I talked to him a lot. Hell, I was drinking

the man's hooch. Didn't understand much he said, but I didn't care. Free hooch is free hooch."

"What'd he talk about?"

"Hell, I don't know. Stuff about how he moved here expecting people to be good country folk but that everybody was stuck up and treated him like crap. Everybody except us Indians, who he understood and were good people. He really got going on that, and before you know it, he's saying that he wants to join the tribe and asking if any of us can arrange that. A couple of the old-timers have this quick conversation in Chippewa and then tell him they'll check into it. So he orders another round. Hell, we kept him going for hours like that. Goddamn white man's got a lot of nuts telling us that crap. If we'd been bad Indians, we'd have rolled him outside, but we just drank his hooch."

"What'd he say about the dogwolf?"

Jim hesitated. "Oh, not much. Same kind of thing he said about people, I guess. That he'd figured it'd be a friend, but that the son of a bitch turned out to be vicious and that he'd shoot it tomorrow if he hadn't promised to look after it."

"Promised who?"

"How would I know? God, the guy was falling-down drunk, and I wasn't doing too bad myself. I was lucky to make that much sense of it." He stretched. "I've got to get going. Too much talk. Us Chippewa are supposed to be strong, silent types, you know."

"Just for the white man."

"Well, enough talk, anyway." He got up.

"What're you up to tomorrow?"

"Not much. You sitting tower or should we go after some squirrels?"

"I'm off, but I've got to do something about our field. That dry grass catches fire, we're going to be in some deep shit."

"So you want this lazy Indian boy to help you cut it."

"That's the idea."

"Guess I could work it in. When do you want to start?"

"Early would be best. Get a start while the dew is still on the grass."

He snorted. "What dew? I haven't seen any dew since May."

"That's because you don't get your lazy ass out of bed early enough."

"Well, I'd better not go to bed tonight, then. Hold the trapdoor for me."

Back on the ground, he waved and then disappeared into the woods. I ate my lunch and sat on the deck through the afternoon, scanning the forest and answering the radio checks. Now and then, the dogwolf howled, and once, far off, I heard the snap of Jim's .22.

Steve called us down half an hour early, and I beat feet for home and supper. I'd come out of the red pine and was starting up the far side of the ridge, thinking about checking again for evidence of the lightning strike, when a sudden rustling in the grass made me lurch back. To the right of the path, two big pine snakes writhed in a ball, tongues darting and scales burring as they mated in the evening heat. I don't like snakes, although I'll pick up the small ones on a dare, which few Chippewa will. None of the snakes around here are poisonous, but the old-time *Anishinaabe* — what people like Aunt Loretta still call the Chippewa — believed that snakes and toads were bad manito, and it's a prejudice that hangs on. I watched them for a couple of minutes, then stepped around, and followed the path over the ridge.

The girls were playing in the yard and Chuck was sitting on the back steps drinking a beer when I got home. He looked exhausted. "Hi," I said. "Put it out?"

"Yeah, we put it out. Stopped it about two hundred yards short of a big jack-pine plantation. If it'd gotten in there, we'd have had a hell of a time."

I sat beside him, and he handed me the beer can — something that Mom gives him hell about. I took a long swallow, the beer cold and sharp in my throat. I handed it back. "Thanks." He nodded, and we sat in silence under the slow rustling of the willow. "I thought I saw the willow catch fire last night just when the storm started. Kind of a blue flame on the tips of the branches. But it didn't burn. Am I nuts, or what?"

He looked at me curiously. "Blue flame?" I nodded. "I'll be damned. I've always wanted to see that. You're lucky."

"See what?"

"It's called Saint Elmo's fire. Sailors see it on masts sometimes, and I've heard of it playing on the branches of tall trees. It's caused by electrical discharge, but it's rare. Very rare." He sat considering. "Funny, though. I thought it was supposed to be yellow."

I felt the comfort of his explanation slipping away from me. "Maybe it was kind of a bluish-yellow. I'm not sure; I'd been watching the lightning and maybe my eyes were a little screwed up."

"Could be. Or maybe it is blue. I'll have to look it up." He took a swallow of the beer. "Jeez, I've always wanted to see that. . . . You superstitious?"

"Not very. Why?"

"Sailors think it's a bad omen."

"How about foresters?"

"We're scientists, we don't have superstitions."

"Why do you knock on wood then?"

"Bad habit. Don't get started on me; I'm tired." He held out the beer can. "Want to kill this?"

"Sure," I said.

I didn't mention the lightning hitting the ridge. Saint Elmo's fire was enough to worry about for one night. Later, I thought about telling him that I planned to cut the field in the morning, but he fell asleep in his armchair after dinner and Mom made him go to bed. Well, Jim and I could handle it, and Chuck would only worry if he knew.

CHAPTER
THREE

The engine of the old International caught on the third try. I let it warm, then dropped the tractor into gear and chugged out of the shed in a cloud of diesel smoke. I backed around to the mower and left the engine idling while I hooked up. The mower's sickle bar could have used some sharpening, but I only planned on cutting a five-acre strip near the buildings. God knows, the hay wouldn't need much drying, and we could bale tomorrow or the next day. I was a little uneasy about going ahead without telling Chuck, but he'd left early, complaining of a headache. Mom had taken the girls shopping in Ashland, and — if Jim ever got his dead ass over here — we could have the job done long before anybody got home.

I was considering starting without him when he came down the drive. He waved, trudged over to the pump house, and stuck his head under the faucet. I sauntered over. "You don't look so good."

"Thanks. I feel worse."

"Where's your heap?"

"Up at Eddy's. I went in for a couple last night, and the damned car wouldn't start when I came out."

"Battery?"

"No, starter, I think." He bent to take a long drink.

"So you went back in."

"Yep. And then I went back in again after it didn't start the second time. After that I kind of forgot about it. Ended up sleeping in the car. Stupid damned Indian anyway. You got a beer?"

I hesitated. Chuck doesn't drink more than two or three a week and was likely to notice. "I guess so. Sure that's what you really need?"

"Believe me, if you had this hangover, you'd try anything."

I got him a beer from the kitchen, and he drank it in the shade with his eyes closed. "You gonna be able to do this?" I asked.

"Yeah, just give me a minute."

I went back to the shed, got an oil can, and hit a few spots on the mower. Jim joined me. "Okay," he said. "I think I'll live."

I refolded the old blanket on the hard seat of the tractor and, with Jim riding beside me, drove out into the field, the sickle bar laying down a brown swath of cut grass behind us. On the fourth or fifth circuit, we must have run over a nest of grass snakes, because suddenly there were snakes everywhere, slithering from under the mower and across the new-mown hay. Beside me, Jim tensed.

51

"Bad manito," I called over the roar of the tractor.

"So they say," he shouted back. "Stop for a minute. I've got to take a leak."

I stopped the tractor and cut the engine to an idle. Jim checked the grass for snakes and hopped off. "Mom said maybe I ought to go into the woods and starve myself for a few days until I get my personal manito," I said.

"What do you think?"

"I think it sounds like a lot of work."

He grunted. "Could be."

"If you could choose your manito, Jim, what would it be?"

"You can't choose them; they choose you."

"Yeah, but if you could?"

"What makes you think I don't have one already?"

"Do you?"

"No. But if I did, I couldn't tell you what it was. That's not allowed."

"Come on, Jim. Stop dodging. What would you choose for a manito?"

He zipped his fly. "I don't know. Bear, I guess."

I laughed. "Like the Hamm's Beer bear on the commercials?"

For a second, anger flashed in his eyes. "Hey, you don't want the answer, don't ask."

Sometimes Jim gets sensitive, so when he climbed back on the tractor, I asked seriously, "Why Bear, Jim?"

"Because of the Hamm's Beer bear. Leave it at that."

"No, really, Jim. I'm sorry I made fun."

He gazed at me, and then shrugged. "Back when my granddad was alive, he told me a few things about the Bear cult. How they made the sweat lodge hotter, stayed in longer, had the deepest visions. Even the members feared what they saw. Said that the lodge itself turned into the insides of Bear. And I guess even if I've never been that brave, I've always wanted to be. You know, to push things to the limit. To take the really big risks."

I didn't reply for a long minute, remembering the old way it's supposed to be when a friend says something deep. "Yes," I said. "I've felt that, too."

Jim looked out across the field toward the green crowns of the forest shimmering in the heat beneath the dull cloud of smoke. "Maybe if . . ." His voice trailed off.

"If what?"

"Oh, hell. I don't know. Come on, let's get this damned hay mown. I could use another beer." I pushed the throttle in and dropped the tractor in gear.

We cut for another hour, neither of us saying much, as the sun beat down and the itching hay dust rose around us. I'd just turned onto the leg closest to the farm when Jim let out a yelp. "Holy shit, there's smoke back there!"

I swung around in the seat just in time to see an

53

orange tongue of flame twist out of the grass. Jim was off the tractor and running back toward the fire. I slammed the tractor into neutral, cut the engine, grabbed the blanket, and ran after him. He was stomping at the fire, but it was spreading much too fast. I threw him the blanket. "I'll get the hose," I yelled. I sprinted for the pump house, praying that together our two hoses would reach.

I had to disconnect the pump-house end of one, drag it across the yard, and screw it to the end of the other. My hands shook, and I bit my lip hard, tasting blood. I ran back to the pump house, spun the faucet full open, and raced for the field, a hundred feet of hose jerking behind me. I could hardly see Jim through the smoke billowing around him, but I could hear him cursing and choking. I hit the end of the hose thirty feet short of the fire. I twisted the nozzle, praying that I hadn't kinked the line. A stream of water shot out, cold and beautiful in the sun. I aimed it into the smoke and heard Jim squawk in surprise. He stumbled out of the smoke. "On me! On me!" he yelled. I doused him from head to foot, the water steaming on his pants. "Good. Good. Now the blanket. . . . Okay, follow me. Work in from the edge."

His head and torso disappeared into the eddying smoke again. I kept the stream low, following the outline of his legs as he beat at the edges of the fire. All the while, a clock ticked in my head: fifteen, at most twenty, minutes of pressure, then the well would need fifteen minutes, maybe longer, to recharge. The smoke started turning gray and then white. I could make out Jim through it, a ghost whipping a sodden blanket against the faltering fire. Just a few more minutes, God. Just a little more water.

Jim stumbled out of the smoke and steam. He bent over, hands on knees, and gagged.

"I think we've got it licked," I called.

He straightened, wiping his mouth on a shirt sleeve. "Yeah, I think so. Wet down the edges real good. The center will burn itself out." He sat down and put his head between his knees. Five minutes later, I had the fire out, just as the stream began to lose pressure.

I turned off the nozzle and went to sit by Jim. He looked at me with bloodshot eyes and grinned crookedly. "We have to be the two dumbest Indians I know," he said.

"I'm half white."

"Maybe that explains it. What the hell happened, anyway?"

"I don't know. Maybe we hit a rock with the sickle bar and threw a spark."

He shook his head. "Whatever happened, we are goddamn lucky. Me, especially. My pants caught a couple of times."

"You get burned?"

"Some, I guess."

"Let's go have a look. There's salve in the house."

"In a minute. Nothing's hurting yet." We sat in

silence, watching the burned circle of grass hiss and steam. "I suppose Mac saw the smoke from the tower," Jim said.

"It'd be pretty hard to miss."

"What's your bet: county, state, or federal?"

"Whoever's got a unit over this way, I guess."

A couple of minutes later, we heard a car bumping down the drive. Jim squinted. "Looks like the state wins. I think that's my buddy Warden Big Bill Caswell coming now."

"Well, it's my fault. I got us into this, so I'll do the talking."

"Oh, Bill's okay. I don't trust him, he doesn't trust me. We get along fine."

Big Bill makes even Chuck look small, which is hard to believe if you've seen Chuck. He got out of his car, surveyed the scene, and shook his head. He thumbed his handset, talked into the radio for a moment, and then walked over to where we sat waiting. He smiled slightly. "You boys got a burn permit?"

"Nope, you got us, Warden." Jim held out his hands. "Slap the cuffs on."

"Don't tempt me, Redwing." He looked at me. "You are?"

"Pete LaSavage."

"I thought so. I knew your dad way back when. You look like him. So, what happened here?"

I shrugged. "We were cutting hay and must have kicked up a spark somehow. It happened fast."

"I'll bet. Either of you smoking?" I shook my

head. "You're lucky. Judge would have your tails for that. Better hose down the grass another time while I write up a report."

I took a breath. "We getting a ticket out of this?"

"I'll try to think of one." He grinned. "No, you're okay. But I'd forget about haying for now." I nodded.

We hosed down the grass again. Big Bill waved us over and handed me a clipboard. "Read it and sign on the bottom if it states accurately what happened." I read it and signed. He got in his car and started the engine. "Take it easy, boys. Better wait until Chuck gets home before you do anything more."

We waved as he drove out of the yard. "I guess if you've got that salve, I'll try some," Jim said.

I got the first-aid kit from the house and helped Jim clean and bandage the angry red burns on his legs. He winced, and I said, "Steady. You full-bloods are supposed to ignore pain."

"My ass," he said. "We're supposed to be smart enough to avoid it. Ouch. Damn it, take it easy."

"That's the last of them. Want another beer?"

"I thought you'd never ask. Sure you won't get in trouble with Chuck or your mom?"

"I guess you've earned it. I figure they're going to be a lot more upset about the fire, anyway."

"How mad they gonna be?"

"Mom's going to have a fit. Hard to tell with Chuck. Just a second and I'll get you that beer."

We sat in the shade of the pump house while Jim drank his beer and I drank a can of Mountain

Dew. Beyond the trees, the dogwolf's howl drifted up into the hot sky. "The son of a bitch is laughing at us," Jim said.

"It's just lonely."

"You're not starting to feel sorry for that damned thing, are you?"

"No."

"Good. Because that *windigo* bastard never loved anybody or anything. It just hates, and it wants out so it can prove just how much."

"You're imagining things. It's just a dog."

"Yeah, maybe. But we'd all be a lot better off if somebody shot it." He handed me the empty can. "I'm going to Eddy's to get my car. Want to come along?"

"That's fifteen miles. How you going to get there?"

"Same way I got here. Stand by the highway and stick out my thumb. What else have I got to do?"

"You could hang around here. I'll run you up there after Mom or Chuck gets home."

"No, you're going to have enough trouble just explaining the fire, and I'd rather miss that scene."

He was limping as he headed down the driveway. "Look after those burns," I called. He waved.

Chuck heard about the fire around that time and came home an hour later. He stood at the edge of the yard, hands on hips, glaring at the burned grass. "Goddamn it," he muttered.

I'd already apologized once, but I did it again. "I'm sorry, Chuck. We were just — "

He waved a hand in disgust. "It's not your fault. If it's anybody's, it's mine. That field should have been cut weeks ago. Well, come on. Let's see if we can get something done before your ma comes home and really blows a gasket."

"What are we going to do?"

"I'm going to rig a fifty-five-gallon barrel on the back of the tractor. That way we'll have water right there if something happens. You probably could have stopped that fire at the start with a few buckets of water."

There isn't a lot that Chuck can't do with angle iron, chain, and a welding torch. In an hour, we had the drum anchored to the rear of the tractor. I filled it at the pump house, while Chuck sharpened the sickle bar. He relaxed a little when we drove out into the field, fifty gallons of water slapping against the sides of the barrel. "How's the steering?" I asked.

"Okay. You can feel the weight, but we've got it pretty well balanced." He swung into the swath of grass where I'd jerked the tractor to a stop. "I'll take it around a couple of times, and then you can have it. I'm going to sit on my butt on the ridge for a while. Maybe catch a few Z's."

"Okay." I hesitated. "I let Jim drink a couple of your beers. He had kind of a rough morning, what with getting singed and everything."

"Well, I guess that was okay. From what I hear, it wouldn't be the first time Jim Redwing had a beer in the morning. Just think twice about joining him. Not a good idea." I nodded.

At the northwest corner of the mowed strip, Chuck stopped the tractor and climbed off. The dogwolf howled just then. Chuck grimaced. "I am giving Wilson about one more day to get home before I do something about that bastard."

"Jim said he saw Wilson up on the north end of the rez last week. Said he was on a real bender."

"Well, that means he's alive, anyway. But so help me, if he isn't home by this weekend, I'm going to shoot that damned dog."

"You already said that. Go catch a nap. I'll howl if I need you."

"Yeah, you do that," he said.

It was dusk by the time Mom and the girls got home from Ashland, and she didn't see the burned patch in the field. Chuck told her about it that evening, and she gave me the silent treatment for a couple of hours. But near bedtime, she said, "Oh, heck, I thought that hay needed cutting, anyway. Day after tomorrow, I'll take the girls to the Sorensons' and then help you bale."

I checked on the dogwolf the next morning on my way to the tower. It was pacing its cage, looking more gaunt than ever. I couldn't see that it had eaten any of the food I'd thrown over the fence, but the water trough was empty. I filled it under the dogwolf's stare, told him to screw himself, and took the trail to the tower.

I'd never known it so still above the treetops. The smoke cloud hung thick and gray over the forest, its odor heavy in the heat. I was early, so I flipped over to the fire-fighting circuit to see if anything was happening. That was a no-no during working hours, but I figured there wasn't any harm before. So far all was quiet with just routine traffic on the circuit. I heard Chuck call in for a diesel mechanic to repair a problem on one of Fire Three's bulldozers. Fire Five's boss called in to complain that his fuel delivery was late and how the hell was he supposed to fight fires without fuel in his equipment? Steve soothed him and then handed over the circuit to Charlie Harik. That meant Steve was about to start checking in the towers, so I switched over, beat the rush, and then moved out onto the deck.

It was ninety-five by eleven o'clock, and my headache was back big time. I sat with my chair leaned back against the shack and my feet on the rail. Between scans of the forest, I closed my eyes, trying to still the red thudding in my temples. The dogwolf howled and howled. Goddamn it, I wasn't just going to kill it, I was going to skin it out and nail its pelt to Wilson's door.

I made a circuit of the deck and then got a wet rag from the shack and sat for a few minutes with it over my eyes. The coolness helped, and my mind wandered over what Mom had told me about the trip from Coeur d'Alene after Dad's accident. What had he really found inside himself in the long hours he'd lain in the back of the pickup staring at the endless Western sky? And was there any of that in me? Or just the emptiness I'd felt all summer?

The radio crackled. "One-One, this is Crescent Lake. Radio check. How you doin', Pete?" I reached through the window for the handset, lifting the binoculars to my eyes with the other hand to give the forest a quick scan. "I'm still here. Nothing going on. You're coming in fine."

"Roger. So are you. Break. One-Two, this is Crescent Lake . . ."

Steve went on checking the other towers. I twisted to put the handset back on the desk, picked up a pencil, and logged the time of the call. I turned back just in time to see a black cloud erupt from a clump of pines a quarter mile to the northeast. My stomach flipped over and for an instant I couldn't breathe. I tried to grab for the handset, but my arm wouldn't move as the cloud folded over on itself and came boiling across the treetops. I was paralyzed, my brain locked halfway between screeching gears. Christ, that wasn't a fire! What the hell was it? My legs came alive and I jumped to my feet. The cloud was rising, aiming right at me. I leaned into the binoculars, trying to get its boiling heart in focus. The blackness filled my field of vision, its edges reaching out, becoming arms, becoming wings, reaching out to embrace me. Shit! Not yet, you bastard! I plunged for the door. My foot hit the overturned chair and I fell, my knee tearing against the steel grating of the deck. I hit the door, threw it shut behind me, and lunged to slam the windows shut as darkness swallowed the tower in a roar of ten billion black wings. I stumbled back and stood in the center of the shack as the cloud shook the tower like driving rain.

In a moment it was past, the cloud rolling south over the trees. The radio crackled. "One-One, this is Crescent Lake. What have you got over there, Pete?"

I picked up the handset with shaking fingers. "This is One-One. Bugs. Billions of the damned things. They came out of some pines so fast that I just got the windows shut in time."

"No fire, then?"

"Nothing. Scared the hell out of me, but no fire."

Another voice broke in. "This is One-Two. I concur with One-One. I can see the cloud from here, heading south-southwest. It's breaking up, whatever the hell it is."

"Roger. Wait one, guys." There was a pause, and then Steve came back on. "This is Crescent Lake. That's a new one on us. Nobody here ever heard of anything like it. I guess things are getting stirred up all over. You okay, Pete?"

"Yeah, I'm okay. I need to go down to get some water to clean the windows."

"Roger. Tell me when you're back up."

I signed off, suddenly aware of the heat inside the closed shack. I pushed open the door and stepped onto the deck. A breeze stirred, cooling me through my sweat-soaked shirt. My knee felt sticky, and I looked down to see the blood soaking through the torn fabric of my jeans. I got the first-aid kit and bandaged the scrape, stood, and flexed the knee. I'd live.

I didn't want to think yet, so I got busy with the water. I emptied what was left in the five-gallon jerry can into a bucket and then lowered the can to the ground on the pulley that hung from a corner of the shack. I climbed down, filled the can at the pump, and climbed back up. It was a cumbersome process with no one on the ground to help, but a lot better than trying to carry the can up the ladder.

Drying insect corpses plastered the wall and window on the north side of the shack. I called in to tell Steve that I was back in the tower, and then set about cleaning up. It was tedious, and I couldn't avoid thinking any longer. Whatever had sent that cloud of insects boiling out of the pines didn't interest me much. Let the foresters at Crescent Lake figure that one out. But I was bothered by my reaction. It'd just been a cloud of bugs, for God's sake. Nothing that anybody with his shit together couldn't have figured out long before it hit the tower. But I hadn't. Instead, I'd been mesmerized by its darkness. What had I imagined was coming to get me? An evil manito? The Thunderbird? Death?

I slumped back against the rail, staring at the dirty circle I'd scrubbed on the wall. I was losing it and losing it fast — seeing too much of what wasn't there, or what was better left unseen. In the trees to the southeast, the dogwolf howled. I shivered, knowing what it wanted — knowing just as surely as I'd known when it howled in the heartbeat before the rain roared out of the trees on the night I'd seen the willow glowing with flame and watched the lightning strike the ridge and rebound in a ball of fire. The dogwolf wanted me to set it loose or to put a bullet through its brain.

I signed off for the day and climbed down from the tower as the sun edged into the trees, its setting blood-red through the smoke from the fires in the forest. A breeze had come up, and the tension cables holding the legs of the tower together thrummed softly as I descended into the still heat of the woods.

Instead of going home, I made my way through the trees toward the pine grove northeast of the tower. The grove was only a mile from our place, but I'd always skirted the low, swampy land surrounding it. It took me a half hour to work my way through the brush, and the shadows were long by the time I reached the edge of a muskeg swamp and had a clear view of the grove again. At the center of the swamp, some glacial twist of fancy had left an island of bedrock. Three tall pines grew out of the north side of the island, their crowns shadowing the granite outcropping at the top.

In a normal summer, muskeg swamps are nearly

impassable, but the drought had dried the muck, and I picked my way across on the lumps of spongy moss. A fresh cloud of mosquitoes and blackflies rose around me with every step, and the heavy air stank of a thousand years of rotting vegetation. I scrambled onto the firm ground at the base of the granite and spent a minute catching my breath and slapping at the mosquitoes and flies.

I studied the granite for the best way to the top and then, no longer remembering quite why I'd come, started the climb. But something seemed to hold me back, and I hesitated halfway up, suddenly spooked by the dark jumble of boulders ahead. This was a place where no one would come in years, maybe decades, and something in the shadows seemed to whisper that bad things could happen if I trespassed here. I leaned back against a lichened boulder and tried to get a grip. Whether I left or climbed higher, nothing would happen here but the ordinary comings and goings of seasons, birds, and animals. The woods were safer than any big city, than most small towns, for that matter. In the fading light, I could trip and break my damn-fool neck, but nothing except my own stupidity was going to hurt me in the rocks. The choice was a rational one: climb higher on the off chance I'd find a clue for the sudden migration of that cloud of insects, or forget it and start walking home while I still had light to spare. I looked again at the boulders, told myself that I'd been stupid enough for one day, and turned back.

I crossed the muskeg, watching my step carefully and telling myself that the prickle I felt on the back of my neck was only sweat. I made it through the hardwoods in the last of the light, hitting an old logging road that brought me out on the county trunk that's the shortcut between the state highway and the tourist towns along Lake Superior. I was beat and turned to stick out my thumb when I heard a car coming down the road from the north. The car slowed, and I thought I had a ride, but then the driver put his foot back on the gas and all I got was a face full of dust and a quick glimpse of a tourist family, kids wide-eyed in the back, as the car blew past. *Look, kids, a real live Indian. I'll slow down so you can get a good look. . . . Can we pick him up, Daddy? . . . No, no. We don't want any trouble. They're all drunks and thieves. Look close now. Okay. I've got to speed up in case he throws something.* Screw you, I thought.

Chuck looked up over his reading glasses when I came into the kitchen. "Hi," he said. "Heard you had another adventure today."

"Yeah, but at least I had witnesses this time. One-Two and a couple of the other towers saw it, too."

"I know. I was in the office. Why didn't you call it in?"

"I was trying to figure out what the hell it was. I knew right away that it wasn't smoke. And then I was too busy getting the door shut and the windows closed. It took me most of the afternoon to clean the bugs off the walls and the windows."

"What kind of bugs were they?"

"Beats me." I took an envelope from my shirt pocket and tossed it on the table. "I thought you'd ask, so I saved you a few." I opened the oven to see what Mom had left me for supper.

Chuck emptied the envelope onto his newspaper and nudged the insect corpses around with his coffee spoon. "Hmm. I've never seen anything like these. Came out of a clump of pines, you said?" I nodded. "Must be some kind of fly, I guess." He funneled the corpses back into the envelope. "I'll show them to Phil Bagley. He'll know."

"Where are Mom and the girls?"

"Staying over at the Sorenson place. Ken's off at some teachers' convention, and Sue's lonely. Janice said she'd be back first thing in the morning to help you with the baling."

"Good," I said. "How'd things go today?"

"Okay. We got a good ditch dug on the northeast corner of the big bog that's been giving us so much trouble. Hit a hot spot where the fire was working into a balsam stand, cut it off, doused it, and then knocked down an acre and a half of trees for good measure. Too bad; they were only two or three years away from market. But if we can hold the line there, it won't be a big loss." He folded his paper and stretched. "I'm going to turn in. Maybe read in bed for a few minutes."

The food had made me feel better, and I was suddenly restless. "Mind if I take the truck over to the rez?"

He looked at me in surprise. "Tonight?"

"It's only a little after nine. I haven't seen anybody for a couple of days, and I'm getting kind of stir-crazy."

"Well, I don't know. . . ."

I knew I had him then, because he usually says no right off if he's going to turn me down. "Come on, Chuck. It's only four miles, and nobody on the rez cares as long as you can see over the steering wheel."

"Well, okay, I guess," he said. "Keep it out of the ditch and get home by midnight or so."

"Thanks." I rinsed my plate and got the keys from the cupboard.

Where the state highway cuts across the southern border of the reservation, a sign reads: "Moon Lake Indian Reserve. Home of the Chippewa Chiefs, Class C State Wrestling Champions, 1966." But on the back route I drove, there was no sign, only the sudden narrowing and roughening of the road as I crossed the line from the township onto the reservation. I drove slowly through the dark heat, watching the ditches for the reflection of deer raising startled eyes at the approach of headlights. There aren't many yard lights on the rez, and you can pass by the outlying houses hardly knowing they're there except for the mailboxes by the road. I stopped at the end of Jim's road, shutting off my headlights to catch any light in the windows of the cabin he shared with John Redwing. Nobody home.

At the junction of the north–south road, I turned right and drove the couple of miles into town. There isn't much to the main street of Moon Lake: the supermarket, the lumberyard, the café, two bars, the post office, the Catholic church, and the trading post where the tourists can buy rubber tomahawks made in Taiwan. The tribal center is on a hill up a side street, and most of the adults go there in the evenings. After the tribe got money to build a new fire station, the committee turned the old station into a youth center. Most of the kids hang out there until they're old enough to get cars and jobs off the reservation. Or, as Jim did, to start hitting the bars at the north end of the lake.

I drove the length of Main Street, looking for Jim's old Dodge, and then parked across from the youth center. Some guys I knew from school were standing near the door, and I stopped to talk for a couple of minutes before stepping inside. It was stuffy, the ceiling fans hardly disturbing the tobacco smoke hanging thick over the pool tables and dance floor. The jukebox was cranked up high, and the pool players had to shout to call their shots. Three or four sweaty couples still had the energy to dance, but most of the other kids were standing in bored knots along the walls. Near me, a group of girls giggled, giving me sidelong glances and hiding their grins behind their hands. After a moment, they parted, pushing a short, pudgy girl through toward me. Mona. Oh-oh, I thought, but it was too late to run.

"Hi, stranger," she said. "Where you been hiding?" She almost had a fit of giggling, but choked it back.

"Hi, Mona. I've been around."

"Haven't seen you."

I shrugged. "I'm easy to miss."

"Not for me. Who you looking for?"

"Jim Redwing."

"Oh, he never comes in here anymore. He's always up at Eddy's getting drunk. What do you want him for?"

"I need some help baling hay tomorrow."

"How much do you pay? I might be available."

"Nothing, and you're not big enough."

She huffed. "I'm as old as you are, even if I am a grade behind."

"You know what I mean."

"Oh, sure. Men's work. I wish I could convince my dad there's such a thing."

"Well, I'll keep you in mind," I said, knowing instantly that I'd made a lousy choice of words.

Her smile disappeared. "That'd be a switch. Has your phone been out of order or something?"

"It's been a busy summer. Hey, I've gotta go, Mona. I'll see you around."

Out on the sidewalk, she caught my arm. "Hey, I'm sorry. Come on, let's get a Coke."

"It's too hot in there, Mona. Too much smoke."

"There's the machine down the block. Come on, I'll buy."

I started to make an excuse, but then let her pull me along. What the hell; Mona was okay. Back in the winter, she'd decided that she wanted me for her guy, and we'd had a few good times until I'd run out of anything to say to her and she hadn't noticed. With the summer, I'd just stayed away, not caring.

At the machine, she started digging in her purse. "I've got it," I said, and dropped some quarters into the machine.

She opened the can I handed her, took a drink, and pushed her long black hair back from her damp forehead. "God, it's hot out here, too."

"Yeah, hot everywhere."

She took my arm, and we started walking. "What do ya wanta do?" she asked.

"I've really gotta go, Mona. My stepdad said to get home early."

She ignored that. "Let's go sit behind the church for a while."

"Really, Mona, I've — "

"Oh, come on. I just want to talk for a few minutes." She pulled me toward the bushes growing behind the Catholic church.

Either Mona can see like a cat, or she'd been there a lot lately. I tripped a couple of times trying to follow her through the shrubbery and then lost her entirely in the darkness. "Here," she whispered, pulling me down beside her. Before I could say anything, she had her arms around me and her mouth clamped on mine. Her tongue tasted of tobacco, and I could feel the sweat on her back through her blouse. I tried to relax, tried to let myself enjoy it. But after a minute, she pulled back. "What's the matter?" she asked.

"Nothing."

"Yes, there is. I can tell. You weren't like this last time."

"I don't know, Mona. It's just — "

She giggled. "Did you forget something? Don't worry, I've got one in my purse." I felt her hand on my thigh. "Remember up in my bedroom last spring when the folks were gone? We sure had fun that afternoon." I didn't reply, and her hand hesitated. "You remember, don't you?"

"Sure," I said.

"Well?" She waited for me to make a move. When I didn't, she took her hand away. "Oh," she said. I heard her dig in her purse, and a moment later, a lighter flared. She drew deeply on the cigarette and let the lighter go out. "What's happened?" she asked.

"A lot. But nothing to do with you and me."

"Nothing's about right. What's the matter? Ain't I good enough for you? I got some white blood, too, you know."

"Oh, that's shit, and you know it, Mona. I never cared one way or the other."

"Yeah? What is it, then? You got some little bitch I don't know about?"

She was about to really piss me off. "No, I don't. But if I did, it wouldn't be any business of yours.

We had some fun a couple of times. There wasn't anything more to it."

"Says you."

"Says me."

She stood up and gave me a sharp kick on the leg. "Well, screw you, you little fag. I wish I hadn't." She stomped off through the shrubs, not caring how much noise she made.

I leaned my head back against the wall of the church. Oh, hell. Why'd I let her bring me here? I'd known it wouldn't work, but I'd gone along anyway. Stupid. After a few minutes, I got up and thrashed my way out of the bushes. I walked along the far side of the street to the pickup. Mona was nowhere in sight. I got in, waved to a couple of the guys still hanging around the door of the youth center, and drove into the darkness beyond the last streetlight. Why hadn't I wanted to make it with Mona? I didn't know, except that I didn't want anything more to do with cages. I turned at the junction and drove west, wishing that I could go on driving forever toward the sliver of moon riding in the still band of clear sky between the trees and the smoke cloud rising from the fires burning deep beneath the forest.

CHAPTER FOUR

I drove the tractor into the field at first light, sweeping the hay into long windrows with the side rake. For half an hour, it was pleasant in the shadow of the ridge, but then the sun rose a venomous orange, the shadows rolling up like poisoned night creatures at its touch. The heat came pulsing across the brown stubble, and I felt the awakening thud of the headache in my temples.

I finished raking in midmorning, hooked up the baler, and then sat for a few minutes in the shadow of the pump house, waiting for Mom. She came out the back door lugging a basket of wet sheets. "Get your lazy Indian carcass over here and help me hang these up," she called.

I levered myself up and went over. "It's a half-white carcass," I said.

"Don't start that again. Here." She handed me the end of a sheet.

We pinned it to the line. "Won't take them long to dry in this heat," I said.

"About a minute and a half. Got the baler and the wagon set to go?"

"Yeah. Ready to do some man's work?"

"Don't give me that garbage. I've thrown a heck of a lot more hay bales then you have, Sonny."

"Better show me how it's done, then."

"Nice try. I'm driving." She pulled a kerchief out of a pocket and tied it over her long black hair. "Ready when you are."

Mom drove the tractor down the windrows while I stood on the swaying wagon, grabbing each bale as it fell from the baler chute and wrestling it onto the stack at the rear. At fifty-five pounds, every bale weighed close to half of what I did, and for a while, I tried to keep track of how many times I'd moved my body's weight. But counting was too much effort in the heat. The sun hammered on my bare back, and I itched all over from hay dust and sweat. I could feel my palms blistering every time I slid a gloved hand under the binder twine to jerk a bale onto my knee for the twist and heave onto the pile. Finally we had a load, and Mom turned the tractor toward the farm. We parked the wagon by the drive, where one of Chuck's customers — if he still had any — could pick up the load.

At the pump-house faucet, Mom filled a cup, and then stood back while I stuck my head under the cold stream. "You look bushed," she said. "Maybe we should let the rest wait a day."

"Let's just get it done. I'm okay."

"All right," she said. "Just don't faint and fall under the wheels."

"I'm not going to faint."

"Good. See that you don't. Or at least whimper or something first."

"Right," I said.

I lost track of time somewhere in the middle of loading the second wagon, and after that I worked in a red haze, my eyes screwed nearly shut by the dust, sweat, and the headache throbbing red and black with my pulse. All the while, the dogwolf howled beyond the trees.

The tractor swung left, and I nearly fell off the wagon, regaining my balance to see Mom heading in toward the farm. "We've got room for a few more," I shouted.

She called back over the tractor's roar, "That's enough for today. I've got to pick up the girls."

I looked at the sun, surprised to see it well down toward the western horizon. I leaned back against the stack of bales and gave in to the red haze for the time it took us to cross the field to the farm.

When we'd unhooked the wagon, she said, "I'm going to change and run. You'd better take a shower. You stink."

"Thanks for telling me."

"What are mothers for?" She grinned.

I backed the baler under the overhang of the shed, parked the tractor, and trudged to the house. Mom came out, tucking a fresh blouse into her jeans. "Back in a bit," she called.

I got some clean clothes from my room, went to the pump house, stripped, and used a bucket to wash. I sat naked on my shirt with my eyes closed, letting the air dry me. My headache throbbed, its beat seeming to quicken every time the dogwolf howled beyond the trees. Enough, goddamn it! I grabbed my clothes and pulled them on.

Inside the garage, where Chuck and I kept our guns, I hesitated, then took down my .308 deer rifle from the rack, leaving my shotgun and .22 where they hung. I loaded it in the yard and then set off for the ridge. By the time I reached the red pine beyond, the dogwolf had stopped howling, and I knew — knew even though it made no sense — that he was waiting.

Crazy as I was that afternoon, I stopped long enough at the edge of the clearing to look for signs of Wilson. Nothing — just heat and stillness and the burning glare of the dogwolf fixed on the spot where I stood in the shadow of the trees. I stepped into the clearing and walked across to the pump, worked the handle, and bent to drink. The dogwolf made no sound, but I could feel him watching, willing. I squatted in the shadow of the shed, the rifle across my knees. The dogwolf stood unmoving in the center of his cage, not flinching from my stare. My temples throbbed, and for a second there seemed an answering flicker of red in the coal-black of his eyes. "All right, you son of a bitch," I muttered. "Here I come."

I leaned my rifle against the wall, crossed to the cage, and threw the heavy bolt. Then I turned my back on him and walked away, hearing the squeak of the gate swinging open a few inches. The blood thudded in my ears, and I could feel the red heat of his glare between my shoulder blades. My feet seemed to move in slow motion, the scuff of my boots a distant sound on the dry earth, but I refused to hurry. At the shed, I picked up my rifle, jacked a shell into the chamber, and turned slowly to level the crosshairs of the scope between those burning eyes. He didn't flinch, and I could feel the seconds tripping off with my pulse. For two minutes, we stood facing each other, and then he came for me with a roar. His shoulder hit the gate, and the dogwolf was loose, a black streak of hate and flashing teeth aimed at my throat. I held the crosshairs on the spot between his eyes, my trigger finger squeezing down on the last millimeter holding the firing pin back. And in that instant, he spun ninety degrees and streaked for the trees on the north side of the clearing. I followed him in the scope, adjusting the angle to take him in the back of the neck whenever my finger squeezed out that last infinitesimal distance. Twenty feet short of the forest, he braced his front legs, stopping so hard that he nearly lost his balance, and for a second I thought I'd shot him. He turned to stare at me. Slowly, I let up the pressure on the trigger and lowered the rifle. For a long minute we gazed at each other. And then he turned away and loped into the woods.

I slept like death, waking when Heidi and Christine started jumping on my bed. "Mom's called you three times," Heidi yelled.

"Yeah, she says you're going to be late," Christine said.

"Get off the bed."

"No," Heidi said. "Mom said to get you up."

"I'm up."

"No, you're not," Christine said. "You're still lying down."

"Yeah," Heidi said. "Mom says this ain't no time to start acting like some good-for-nothin' Injun."

"I'm going to count to ten," I said, and started counting. They giggled and ran off. I dragged myself out of bed.

Mom shoved a sack lunch at me when I came into the kitchen. "You've only got time for a bowl of cereal." I grunted and sat at the table. "It's going to be hot again today," she said, as if that was news.

"When'd Chuck leave?"

"He got a call at five. The fire in the big bog is trying to get into that balsam stand again. It's the most dangerous place in his sector, and he thinks they might have to knock down another four or five acres just to be sure this time." I nodded, scooped up the last of my cereal, and got up to go. "Be careful," she said.

I paused at the door. "Are they still going to have that rain dance on Sunday?"

"As far as I know. Since when do you care?"

I shrugged. "As you said, anything that works."

In the tower, I checked to see if Mac had left anything in the log for me, and then settled myself for another long day. I replayed the afternoon before, wondering why I'd let the dogwolf go. I'd felt no sympathy for him in his cage, never thought of him as more than a big, vicious mongrel, too stupid to do anybody any good. I'd given him his chance at me, walked away from the cage with my back to him, and he'd been too dumb to take it. Too dumb or too cowardly. Nor had I felt any change of heart tracking him in the scope as he'd bolted for the woods. If I'd felt anything, it was disappointment that he hadn't kept coming at me so that I could have nailed him the second his feet left the ground for the lunge at my throat. Bang, you're dead.

I played the scene through again, freezing the picture at the point where he'd stopped and turned to stare back at me. There'd been nothing in his eyes — no gratitude, no challenge, not even curiosity. Well, that was fine with me. If there ever was a next time, I'd kill him without a thought. I stood. To hell with it. The bastard was gone now, and maybe we could all get a decent night's sleep for a change.

I made a circuit of the deck to check for smoke

in the other directions. Back in my chair, I fixed the binoculars on the forest and let my mind wander. In the distance the sun glinted on the patch of Crescent Lake visible through the trees. I moved the glasses a few inches to the right and studied the broad rectangle of forest that was Chuck's sector and where, a long time ago, my father had found a lonely place to die.

If I'd been Dad, would I have gone there when life no longer seemed worth the pain? I imagined him driving the pickup along the lonely fire lanes and then wrestling it over the ruts of the abandoned logging road to the far corner of that huge block of pine forest that was now the responsibility of a man he'd never known but who slept with his widow and raised his kid. Why had he driven so deep into the forest, and why had he gone through the agony of dragging himself God only knew how far beyond the point where the pickup bogged down? No one had ever said so to me, but I'd always figured that he took a gun along so that he wouldn't have to wait too long in the loneliness for death. On that muddy logging road, he'd already had all the privacy, all the loneliness he needed. What difference if the search parties found his body? Why leave any doubt for the living, when no one would ever blame him for wanting to die? Not Mom, not even me.

I turned in my chair, focusing on the grove of pines thrusting out of the swamp northeast of the tower. I studied it, recalling that black cloud of insects exploding out of the pines like oily smoke. I'd have gone there, crossing the muskeg and climbing up among the boulders under the shadow of the three tall pines. And in the rocks, I would have waited until it was very late, the moon high, and everything asleep except for the stars, the owls, and the little frightened things scuttling in the shadows. I'd sink into that night, not thinking at all, just waiting until the time was right to put the gun —

A dark shape moved in the trees a hundred yards from the tower. I sat bolt upright, my heart hammering. I tried to find the shape again with the glasses, missed it, and then got it on the swing back. I let out the breath that I'd been holding it seemed forever. Only Jim. Get a grip, I told myself.

Jim came into the clearing, waved, and started to climb the ladder. I went inside, got down another coffee cup, and lifted the trapdoor for him. He grunted a hello, accepted the coffee, and walked out onto the deck without another word. I filled my own cup and followed. I gave the forest a quick scan, while Jim sat and sipped moodily at his coffee. "It's gone," he said.

"What?"

"The dogwolf."

"Yes, I know."

"That damned thing is going to be big trouble."

"Oh, I doubt it. It doesn't know how to hunt. It'll probably wander onto the highway and get run

83

over. Or else it'll start raiding garbage cans and somebody will blow it away with a 12-gauge."

"You're wrong," he said. "That thing is a lot smarter than you think."

I snorted. "How do you figure that, Jim? It's been cooped up in that cage for years."

"Yeah, but how about before?"

"It couldn't have learned much; it isn't that old."

"Maybe not, but it remembers way, way back."

"What do you mean? Primal stuff? Things in the genes?"

He looked at me with irritation. "Maybe that's how they explain it in school. All I know is that it remembers."

"Not enough," I said. "It's dumb."

He stared at me and then turned away to gaze over the treetops toward the forest. "Well, I know one thing for sure, I'm going to start carrying my shotgun again."

"You'll get in trouble. Big Bill catches you carrying a shotgun and he'll have your ass."

"I'll take my chances with him rather than that dogwolf." He drained the last of his coffee. "I gotta go."

He paused with his foot on the top rung of the ladder. "Did you do it?"

"Do what?"

"Set it loose."

I looked him in the eye and lied. "Not guilty, warden."

"Good. Because whoever did is going to have a lot to answer for when this is all over."

"You're imagining things," I said. He shook his head and disappeared through the trapdoor.

Twice that afternoon, I took sightings on smoke and called them in. I figured the first for a ditch fire caused by a cigarette thrown from a car. Half an hour later, Steve confirmed my guess, grousing about stupid tourists who ignored all the Forest Service signs and radio announcements.

The second fire was scarier, coming out of the trees on the southern edge of the forest in a sudden pillar of black smoke. I called it in only seconds ahead of two other towers, and then watched as the spotter plane came in fast from the north, dropping to the treetops for a look. A few minutes later, Steve was back on the radio, laughing. "Some old lady is burning shingles in a barrel. She waved at the plane. She's not going to be so friendly when Crazy Horse shows up to lay a ticket on her for breaking the fire restrictions and burning pollutants, too." There were a couple of hoots from bored tower jockeys, and I winced thinking of Bert Weathers, the big sheriff's deputy everybody called Crazy Horse. Stella keyed her mike. "Oh God, Steve, you didn't send Crazy Horse, did you? Give the old girl a break."

Steve laughed. "Nothin' I could do about it, Godmother. He was the closest, and he said he was in the ticket-writing mood." A couple of the other tower jockeys wanted to join in with Crazy Horse stories, but Steve cut them off. "Okay, enough talk, guys. Back to work. The big one's still waiting to chew us up, and we want to see it coming first." The chatter settled, replaced by the low hiss of the static. I tilted my chair back against the wall of the shack and gave the forest a slow scan. Chuck had said that the big one would come down on us like the end of the world. But maybe that Kiowa shaman would come first to save us all.

Storm clouds started building in the southwest about three, and the occasional talk on the radio took on an edge of tension. By the time I signed off and climbed down, a wind was rippling the treetops and thrumming the stress cables of the tower. A flock of goldfinches swept by, dipping and rising like a fluttering blanket of yellow and black. Coming down the last dozen feet, I startled a doe and two fawns browsing in the hollow beyond the clearing. They leaped away, crashing through the undergrowth, their snorts loud in the dull heat.

Chuck was finishing his supper when I came in. "How's it look?" he asked.

"Something's coming. I couldn't tell how bad. Steve said the forecast has the nasty stuff sliding past to the south, but Two-One and Two-Two over on the west said it looks like it's heading straight for us."

"I know where Two-One and Two-Two are," he snapped.

"Sorry."

He waved a hand in disgust. "Ignore me. I'm just tired."

"Sure," I said.

Mom put a plate of stew in front of me. "Are you going to go in?" she asked him.

"I guess I'd better," he said.

Heidi and Christine popped their heads out from under the table and shouted, "Boo."

"Boo yourselves," I said.

They scrambled out. "You didn't see us hiding there," Heidi said accusingly. "How come you're not scared?"

"Yeah, you're supposed to be scared," Christine said.

"I'm scared," I said. "Now let me eat."

"Will you play hide-and-seek with us after dinner?" Heidi asked. "Momma said she would."

"I'll think about it."

Chuck looked out the window, frowning. "You know, I haven't heard that beast of Wilson's howling. It usually howls like crazy when a storm's coming."

"It's not there," I said.

He stared at me. "What?"

"It's not there. I checked."

"When?"

"This morning," I lied.

Mom had turned from the sink. "Oh, Lord," she said. "You don't mean somebody let it out?"

87

"Looks like it," I said. "There's no sign of Wilson."

Chuck slapped a palm on the table, rattling the dishes. "Goddamn it. What damned fool did that?"

"Daddy swore," Heidi said.

"Two times," Christine said.

"Hush," Mom said.

I shrugged. "I don't know. Somebody who felt sorry for it, I guess. I didn't. As a matter of fact, I was thinking of shooting it."

"How about Jim Redwing?" Chuck asked.

I shook my head. "Not a chance; he's scared of it."

Chuck took out his pipe and started angrily loading the bowl. "That damned thing is big enough to pull down a horse. A deer won't have a chance."

"I'm more concerned about the girls," Mom said. "And Pete."

Chuck shook his head. "That's just storybook stuff. Healthy animals don't attack people. No animals around here, anyway."

"I know," she said. "But there's something strange about that animal. I've thought from the first that it was unnatural."

"It's just a dog, Janice," Chuck said. "All that stuff about it being part wolf is just bunk. Dogs and wolves almost never mate in the wild. Put them in a kennel together under just the right circumstances, it can happen, but I'd bet my life that's just a dog."

88

"A big, stupid one," I added. "It'll starve or get hit on the highway."

Mom looked unconvinced, but she turned to washing the supper dishes. Chuck lit a match and pulled moodily on his pipe. "If you're going to smoke that thing, take it outside," Mom said.

He took it out of his mouth and stared at it with distaste. "Sorry. Well, I've got to get going, anyway."

"Call if you're going to spend the night," Mom said.

"If I get the chance. There won't be much time if we get something hot."

He left, and we heard him start the Bronco. Heidi asked, "Momma, can you play hide-and-seek with us now?"

"Yeah," Christine said. "You promised."

"All right," she said. "Pete, will you finish the dishes, please?"

"Sure," I said.

Later, I thought of asking Mom if I could take the truck over to the rez, but I was tired and afraid that I'd run into Mona. She'd still be pissed. Or worse yet, maybe she wouldn't be, and then I'd have to figure out whether I wanted to go behind the church with her again or let her start telling people that I'd lost my balls. I went to bed early, but I couldn't sleep and lay in the heat listening to the 18-wheelers down-shifting to take the big hill on the highway. At last I dozed, coming awake deep in the night as thunder rolled out of the west and over the forest. The phone rang, and I heard Mom talking: "Yes. . . . All right. . . . No, everything's fine here. . . . Be careful. . . . I love you, too."

Chuck was washing the soot off his face and hands at the pump-house trough when I came out in the early light. "Bad night?" I asked.

"Not too bad. We got enough wind to kick up the fire near the balsam stand, but we had it beaten down in a couple of hours. The lightning gave the boys in sector five a hard time, so we took an extra pumper over there around four." He hesitated. "I came home the back way past the rez. Ran into your buddy Jim Redwing. He'd put his car in the ditch and was stumbling around on the road drunk as a skunk. I gave him a ride home."

I grimaced. "Thanks. I'm sure he appreciated it."

"Yeah, well, I've always liked Jim. But next time I'm going to call the sheriff on the radio. I don't want to get Jim in trouble, but if he keeps driving drunk, he's going to kill himself. And there's a damned good chance he's going to take somebody else with him. You remember that crash a couple of years ago when that drunk ran into a station wagon over on the rez? Killed the whole family. Parents and four or five kids."

"I remember," I said. "But he wasn't an Indian. Wasn't he some white duck hunter?"

"Yes, he was white. And the family was Indian. But it doesn't make any difference. Red or white, a drunk's a drunk, and those kids are just as dead no matter what color they were." He toweled his face and hands. "Look, maybe we ought to talk about this. The truth is that Indians have a real problem with alcohol. Even more than whites. Some people may call me a racist for saying that, but I've seen the statistics. Maybe it's something to do with all the crap they've gone through. Or maybe it's something in the genes. I don't know. But I do know that Jim is one Indian kid headed for some very big trouble."

I nodded. "I know. I've tried to talk to him, but it's not easy."

"I'm sure it isn't. Look, all I'm trying to say is that I don't want you riding with Jim when he's been drinking. I don't care what time it is, call me. Even if you've had a few yourself."

"Sure."

"I mean it, Pete. I give a major damn about you, even if I'm only your stepdad."

I felt a sudden lump in my throat. "I know. I, uh, give a damn about you, too. I worry."

It was awkward for us. He took out his pipe and made a show of getting it going. "Don't worry about me," he said. "We'll get through this summer, somehow. Just keep looking after things around here. You did a nice job cutting the hay."

"Once I stopped trying to burn the place down."

He chuckled. "Yeah, well, that wasn't really your fault. Hey, I'm hungry. Do you suppose your ma's got breakfast on?"

At that moment, I almost told him that I'd let the dogwolf loose. But I couldn't — couldn't because I didn't know how to tell him that something in the heat and the smoke beating down the summer told me that it had to be this way. That we were all caught up in something that we didn't understand, and that the dogwolf was a piece of the pattern, a part of the reason that everything was going to hell. And I knew that I was going crazy but that there wasn't a damned thing I could do about it until I found out what was on the other side of the red haze throbbing behind my eyes.

CHAPTER FIVE

I spent the morning hacking at the dry weeds around the outbuildings with a brush hook. When I came in for lunch, Mom said, "Do you want to go over to the rez this afternoon? I need groceries, and Chuck wants some tar paper and shingles for the roof of the toolshed."

"When is he going to have time to roof the toolshed?"

"He's looking ahead, I guess. The fire danger can't last forever."

"We hope," I said.

"We know. Stop being a pill. Do you want to go or not?"

"I guess. Beats brushing."

"Okay," she said. "Girls, come get some lunch. Then we're going shopping."

They came charging in from the living room. "Are we going to see Aunt Loretta?" Heidi yelled.

"Of course."

"Yay," Christine yelled.

"I don't like this soup," Heidi said. "Can I have a sandwich?"

I rode in the back of the pickup while Mom drove and the girls bickered. Except for the smoke haze, there wasn't a cloud in the sky, and I pulled my cap down over my eyes against the glare. Mom took the main highway that cuts across the southern tip of the reservation on its way east to Ironwood and the Upper Peninsula. The pickup doesn't go very fast, and cars kept passing us. A Dodge minivan with Illinois plates came up fast, the driver not even slowing until he was so close that I could guess the color of his eyes below his blond hair. His wife turned in her seat to say something to the kids in back. They leaned forward, mouths open. The minivan hung on our bumper, and then swung out to pass, the kids gawking at me and then pointing excitedly at Mom. Tourists observing the native wildlife.

We were just about to the edge of the reservation when a big Buick swooped past, a cigarette butt flying out the driver's window into the grass at the side of road. Oh, hell. I knocked on the cab window. "Better stop, Mom," I called. She swung over onto the narrow shoulder.

"What's the matter?"

"That jerk tossed a cigarette out the window. I saw it land in the grass. Back up. I'll tell you when to stop."

I stood while she backed up slowly. When I saw

94

the rising wisp of smoke, I knocked on the window again. "This'll do," I called. She stopped, and I hopped over the side of the pickup. Sure enough, the butt lay smoldering in a thatch of brown grass. I ground it under my heel; if the lightning didn't get us one of these nights, the idiots would.

We turned north, following the blacktop into Moon Lake. The town was busy on Friday afternoon with reservation folk in to shop and tourists gawking from their overloaded minivans and station wagons. At the grocery store, Mom handed me Chuck's list. "You might as well go over to the lumberyard while I shop."

"Okay," I said.

Ade Halfaday was filling orders for the six or seven people standing in line at the counter. I'd helped out around the yard on a few Saturdays and knew where everything was, so I got ten pounds of roofing nails and a bucket of tar, waved to Ade, and drove back to the sheds to get the tar paper and shingles. Back in the office, I filled out my slip, signed it, and pushed it across the counter to Ade when there was a break in the rush. "Could use you for a couple of hours if you've got the time," Ade said.

"Sorry. I've got to pick up Mom and my sisters."

"How about tomorrow?"

"Sitting tower. Why not ask Jim Redwing?"

He snorted. "I need a sober Indian." He glanced through the window into the back of the pickup. "Got everything?"

"Yep."

"Okay." He tore off the bottom copy and handed it to me. "Thanks. I'll send the bill to Chuck." He turned to the next person in line.

Back at the grocery store, I got out and sat on the tailgate to wait for Mom. The noon rush was beginning to ease, but Triple, the three-legged town dog, and a couple of his buddies were still doing a good business begging handouts from the tourists going into the trading post. Old Harney was posing for pictures in his rocker at the end of the porch. He scowled at the dogs, sensing competition. When no one was looking, he produced a stone from a pocket in his deerskins and fired it at Triple. He missed, but the ricochet got one of Triple's buddies on the nose. He yelped and the three of them beat it. Harney leaned back with a smile of satisfaction. Another hour, and he'd have the cash to get out of the heat and into one of the air-conditioned bars. He caught me watching him and waved me over. I glanced to see if Mom was in the checkout line yet and then crossed the street.

"Hey, scout, how ya been?"

"Okay, Harney. How about you?"

"Could be better, could be worse. Business is slow. I told the committee that we ought to advertise this rain dance on Sunday, but Strawback and a couple of the others don't want any tourists watching. Say it'll mess up the medicine."

"What do you think?"

He shrugged. "I don't figure that Kiowa's got

much for medicine if a few tourists can mess it up. The way I see it, as long as these white people want to take my picture and buy rubber tomahawks in the store, why not bring in as many as we can?" He rocked, staring dreamily at the street. "What we really need is a casino. Hot damn, would that bring in the tourists. I'd have to incorporate and put on shifts. Hell, I wouldn't sit out here at all except on special occasions. I'd just manage."

I grinned. "You sound part white yourself."

"Full-blood Norveijen on my granddad's side. That's where the Harney comes from."

"I never knew. I figured you for a full-blood. You look it."

"The sun burned out the white a long time ago." He appraised a station wagon coming slowly down the street. "That's a likely looking bunch. Act respectful, scout. Young brave asking advice of wise old chief."

"Okay," I said. "What's the advice?"

"Never pry a bagel out of a toaster with a fork, and never stick your richard in a white woman. Neither's worth the risk."

"Thanks," I said.

"You're welcome." The station wagon parked. He grunted with satisfaction. "Spotted me. . . . So, I was talking to Jimmy Redwing last night. He said you've got trouble with old Wilson's wolfdog."

"No trouble, really. Somebody let it out, that's all."

"I've never seen it. Jim made it sound like it's the size of a bear."

"It's big, but not that big."

Harney chuckled. "Well, I hope it causes some trouble. That'll keep Big Bill busy while us self-respecting Chippewa get on with a little poaching."

"Better not talk that way."

He laughed. "Why? Because of the committee's spies? Hell, half those guys got venison in the freezer already. The committee's fighting a losing battle." The tourist family was out of the car and headed our way, looking uncertain. Harney straightened in his rocker. "Well, time to look the part." He farted with a grunt, and winked at me. I gave him a grin and hopped off the porch before the tourists could unlimber their cameras. Harney looked sternly at them and pointed to the sign near his feet: PICTURES SOLD FOR THE BENEFIT OF THE CHIEF JOE HARNEY INDIAN RELIEF FUND. $5.

I helped Mom load the groceries in the back of the pickup, and we drove over to Aunt Loretta's. Aunt Loretta is actually my great-aunt, and she's old, nearly ninety. She lives in one of the concrete-block bungalows built by the Bureau of Indian Affairs in the fifties. A lot of them look like hell, but she's taken good care of hers. She's taken good care of most things in her life, even when the going got tough. Aunt Loretta was well past sixty, with grandchildren of her own, when Mom's mother died and her father went off to drink himself to death in Minneapolis. Mom was twelve and admits to being a "handful," but Aunt Loretta took her in and, as Mom says, "Kept me out of trouble until your dad came along."

Aunt Loretta met us at the door, looking tiny and incredibly old. "Oh, Aunt Loretta," Mom said, "you didn't have to get up."

"Don't be foolish, *nindaanis*," she said, calling Mom "daughter." "I need excuses to get up." She embraced Mom and the girls, and then put a gnarled hand to my cheek. "Peter is too old to hug now. Except by girls his own age." She gave her whispery laugh, and her milky eyes twinkled. "Many girls, probably. You look like the devil your mother couldn't resist." Mom laughed, and I blushed. Aunt Loretta took her arm. "I embarrass the boy. Come, it's cooler by the window, and I have iced tea for us."

"Why aren't you running that air conditioner Chuck bought for you?" Mom asked.

She chuckled, patting Mom's arm. "I do when it gets too hot. Most of the time the heat feels good to these old bones. It takes more to warm you when you're so old."

I stepped into the kitchen to put our frozen food in Aunt Loretta's freezer until we were ready to go home. When I got to the living room, the girls were already deep into the yarn basket, busily unpacking and sorting the skeins. I sat down next to Mom, who was sitting close to Aunt Loretta to hear her better. They were talking *Anishinaabe*, and I could make out only a word now and then. After a few minutes, Aunt Loretta looked at me. "And how is it with you, Peter? Your mother says you are quiet this summer."

I shrugged. "It's the heat."

"And growing to be a man," she said.

I shifted uncomfortably. "Yeah, some of that, too, I guess."

She nodded. "Every *Oshkinawe* has a summer like that." She looked at Mom. "Tell him to go be with friends. He doesn't want to listen to women gabbling like geese in talk he doesn't understand."

Mom gave me a cool look. "It wouldn't hurt him to learn a little bit of the old talk."

Aunt Loretta touched her arm. "Another time, dear. Tell him it's all right to go now."

Mom tightened her lips, and then made a movement with her head. "Go ahead. Come back in an hour."

I left, happy to be out of the hot room and away from the whispers of age and things that I could not understand, could never know, because I was not Indian enough and had been born too late to learn.

I wandered through the side streets to the center of town. Harney was gone from the trading-post porch, and the heat had emptied the street except for a few disconsolate tourists trying to decide if they'd seen enough of a real reservation before heading for Bayfield, Ashland, Hayward, or Minocqua, where they could get a decent meal and buy Taiwanese rubber tomahawks without the hassle of actually dealing with Indians. Triple and his buddies lay in the hollows they'd scratched in the hard ground on the shady side of the trading post. One of the younger dogs raised his head to gaze at me, but Triple didn't even open his eyes. He could sense the difference between a tourist and a Chippewa boy and knew better than to waste his time in looking pitiful for me.

Billy Twodeer was sitting on the bench outside the youth center, drinking from a large plastic cup. "Hi, Pete."

"Hi," I said, sitting down beside him.

He held out the cup to me. "Want some?"

"Beer?" I asked.

"I wish. The committee's got another bug up its ass: no more beer-drinking on Main Street. Makes us look bad to the tourists. They're hiring another constable to help enforce the ordinance."

"Not a bad idea, maybe."

"Shit. Isn't that what the tourists expect? Bunch of drunken Indians? Jim Redwing's living up to it, that's for sure. Put his car in the ditch again the other night."

"Yeah, I heard."

"Damned fool is going to kill himself. He is way over the line. . . . Say, Mona's got the hatchet out for you. Says if you don't get rid of your new girl and start treating her good, she's going to tell everybody what a shit you are."

"I'm scared," I said.

"Yeah, well, that's what she says. Who's the new girl?"

"There isn't one; she's just imagining things. Besides, Mona wasn't my girl, no matter what she thought."

Billy grunted. "Well, she ain't got over thinking it."

"She'll find somebody else."

"Always has. . . . Got any money you want to lose shooting pool?"

I glanced at the sun. "No money, but I've got a little time."

"Hardly worth the trouble if you ain't got money." He drained the cup. "But, what the hell, I'll shoot you for the cost of the rack."

I lost two games to Billy and then walked back to Aunt Loretta's. Mom and I carried the frozen stuff to the truck, while the girls stood on the steps babbling to Aunt Loretta. "She's going to dance," Mom whispered.

"Aunt Loretta? You're kidding."

Mom shook her head. "She hasn't danced in twenty years, but she's going to dance Sunday."

"Why?"

"Because she thinks this may be the last chance."

"Because she's going to die?"

"No, because she thinks if we don't get rain, there may not be any reservation or any tribe left come fall. That the fire will come and burn everything. She called it the beast, and the way she talked scared me." I stared at her, the keys to the truck forgotten in my hand. She reached out and took them. "So, I'm going to dance, too. I've got to." She turned. "Come on, girls. It's time to go."

As we turned out of the driveway, Aunt Loretta waved and called out in that way that Chippewa women have — the way that I can never understand — of saying something that carries soft over distance: "Walk in beauty, Peter."

Chuck was as surprised as I'd been to hear that Mom and Aunt Loretta planned to dance. But it was an Indian thing, and he just nodded. The girls wanted to dance, too, and Mom promised she'd call around to see if any cousins had old costumes to fit them. She'd looked at me once, but didn't bother to ask if I wanted to dance. Hell, I could hardly keep a beat, and I sure as hell wasn't going to get dressed in a bunch of feathers for a crowd of gawking tourists. And they'd be there, surer than hell.

I spent Saturday in the tower, gazing at the forest and the outline of the clouds drifting above the smoke haze. I watched for Jim, hoping he'd come by the tower to break the monotony. Maybe I'd offer to buy enough gas for us to go to Ashland after I'd put in my time. We could see a movie and cruise for some girls. Most important of all, we could get away from here for a few hours. But he didn't come by, and I knew that he'd probably make an excuse anyway.

Jim didn't get along well with towns. We'd

driven to Ashland on a Saturday in early June with Mona and Billy Twodeer's sister, Sonia. We figured that there wouldn't be many tourists around that early in the season, but they were there in force. We parked on a back street behind a Winnebago camper about a half block long. Jim and I walked around it. "Just get a load of this thing," Jim said. "Shit, where do they get off naming it after an Indian tribe? No Winnebago ever needed something like this to go camping."

Sonia fiddled with her camera, shot a picture of us standing in front of the camper, and then called, "Come on, guys. Let's go shopping."

"Too many tourists down there," Jim said. "I think I'll walk over to the marina and look at the boats."

"Oh, come on, Jim," she said. "Just ignore them."

"I think they're funny," Mona said. "Just a lot of walking sunburn."

Jim grumbled, but came along. The girls dragged us into one shop after another. They didn't plan on buying anything — hell, they had even less money than we did — but they wanted to try on as much as they could. They'd paw through the racks of clothes and then run off giggling to the changing room to come out a couple of minutes later to model for us. I was getting pretty bored by the time we reached the fourth or fifth shop, and maybe that's why I didn't notice that the place had a bad feel to it. Jim and I were standing over by some hats and cowboy boots, while the girls worked their way through a rack of dresses. "I'm hungry," I said. "Let's go get a burger after this."

"Sounds good," Jim said. He idly picked up a cowboy hat and started to try it on.

"Hey, you!" We turned to see the shop owner glaring at us. "Don't put that on your greasy head, chief. Somebody might want to buy it."

It was dead silent as half a dozen tourists looked over at us. Jim put down the hat slowly and, without a word, walked out the door. The girls and I followed, very conscious of all the stares. Outside, Mona whimpered, and Sonia put an arm around her. I hurried to catch up with Jim. After a block, I said, "Screw him, Jim. He's just a goddamn bigot. Forget it."

"Yeah, well, you look almost white, so I guess you can't know how it feels." I didn't say anything and, after another block, he touched me lightly on the shoulder. "Forget that," he said. "It just hurt, that's all."

"Sure," I said. "Hey, let's drive over east. There's a wayside where we can go for a walk on the beach."

He nodded.

The girls didn't need any persuading, and we drove out to the wayside. We walked for an hour on the rocky beach in the wind blowing off Lake Superior. I suggested that we make a driftwood fire and roast some hot dogs. Jim held out the keys to his heap. "You guys can go get the stuff. I'm not going into town again."

"I can't drive up here, Jim. I don't have a license."

"I've got one," Sonia said, and Jim handed her the keys.

We left him sitting on the beach, staring north across *kitchigami* where his ancestors had paddled war canoes but that now lay empty except for a smudge of smoke from an ore boat beyond the horizon where gray sky and gray water met.

Heidi and Christine came bouncing across the lawn in their doeskin dresses. "Daddy what are these called, again?" Heidi asked, fingering the white shells on her dress.

"*Migis* shells. Don't pull too hard on them."

"She's got more than me," Christine complained.

"Well, you've got more beads, then," Chuck said.

"Do not," Heidi said.

"Do, too. And mine are prettier."

"Girls, that's enough," he said. "Come on, get in the truck." He helped them get buckled in.

Mom came out of the house, still fussing with her costume. "You look great, Mom," I said.

She grumbled. "Look better if I hadn't put five or ten pounds on my butt last winter."

Chuck grinned. "Nah, you look just right. Come over here and lay one on me, squaw."

"I'll lay one on you all right," she growled. "Just drive the truck. Come on, we're running late."

The traffic was heavy even on the back way into town, and cars and minivans overflowed the parking lot near the dance ground. Chuck braked the Bronco to let a family of white folks scurry across in front of us, parents dragging reluctant kids toward the crowd of tourists already jostling for the best view.

"Well," I said, "so much for the committee trying to keep this one quiet."

Chuck grunted. "No surprise, there. Too much money to be made from the tourists. Hell, there was even an ad on the radio."

"Daddy swore," Heidi announced from the back.

"Yeah," Christine said. "That's not nice, Daddy."

"Hush," Mom said. "Chuck, just let us off near the pavilion. I want to find Aunt Loretta. She shouldn't be out in this sun too long."

"She knows enough to find some shade, Jan," Chuck said. "Stop worrying." He slowed to a stop again. "This is about as close as we're going to get. Okay, be careful, girls. Parking lots full of tourists are the most dangerous places in the world." Mom and the girls climbed out of the back. "You go along," he said to me. "I'll see you over by the pavilion in a few minutes."

I followed a little distance behind as Mom led the girls through the crowd. Tourists caught sight of them, oohed, aahed, and tried to get their cameras unlimbered in time. Heidi and Christine looked around wide-eyed, but Mom kept her eyes straight ahead, her face set. One potbellied bozo elbowed his way through to get in front of them and started backing through the crowd, his video camera pointed in their faces. Mom swung a little to the left, screwing up his angle, and then more abruptly back to the right so that he ran ass-end into a fat couple horsing down sandwiches and gulping cans of pop. Way to go, Mom, I thought, as she escaped with the girls through a sudden commotion of spilled drinks, yelps of surprise, fumbled sandwiches, and mucho apologies.

The three town constables were fighting to keep the side of the circle nearest the pavilion free of tourists while the dancers got ready. "You take the girls," Mom said. "I've got to find Aunt Loretta."

"But, Momma, we want to dance," Heidi whined.

"A little later on; the big people dance first. Now mind your brother."

I took their hands, wondering how they'd managed to get their fingers sticky already, and led them into the shade of the pavilion. Chuck showed up a few minutes later, striding tall and blond through the knots of Indians adjusting their costumes and ignoring the occasional tourist who slipped past the constables to take pictures. He shook his head. "Must be three hundred tourists with more coming. Regular powwow."

I let him take the girls, who immediately started complaining that they wanted to dance with the big people. "I'm going to see if I can find Jim," I said. "I'll see you later."

"Don't get trampled," he said.

I wandered through the crowd. Triple and his

108

buddies were there, begging sympathy and handouts. Harney was mugging for pictures. The new
Catholic priest, all arms and angles and smiles, was
flapping around, his Nikon's motor drive chattering
like some frenzied stork. And, because even dumb
Indians respond to the profit motive, a dozen local
entrepreneurs were selling cans of beer and pop
from coolers, committee be damned. No Jim.

An amplifier squeaked, and I heard Frank
Yellowhorse, the committee chairman, asking for
everybody's attention. The crowd quieted expect-
antly. Frank took a few steps into the dance circle,
looking uncomfortable. "Uh, we are happy to see
so many of our friends here today. We would like
to ask everyone to be quietly respectful and to
refrain from taking pictures during the first part of
the dance. We are making medicine for rain, and
I think everyone can appreciate just exactly how
badly we need rain. So we ask your cooperation
in preserving the spirit of the ceremony." He
glanced back at the handful of grim-faced committee members standing at the edge of the circle.
"So, uh, thank you for coming. We'll start in a few
minutes."

A couple of Indian men I didn't recognize stood
near me. Maybe they were from Lac Courte
Oreilles or Lac du Flambeau, the big reservations
to the south. One of them snorted. "No pictures?
Fat chance. Might as well ask the *chemokes* to cut
off their hands. They live to take pictures."

The other shrugged. "Well, he had to ask."

I worked my way back to the pavilion and found a place in the crowd of reservation folk. Many of them were kids I knew from school who, like me, had never learned the dances and the chants. They were joking about the tourists, planning the rest of the day, and telling how some of their parents had groused about them not wanting to dance. But it was uncomfortable, edgy talk. Even those of us who didn't like to admit it still believed enough in the medicine to worry about something going wrong.

A buzz ran through the crowd as John Redwing led the singers from behind the pavilion toward the drums at the edge of the circle. He gave the singers a minute to find their places and then brought down his heavy drumstick on the taut deerskin. The chant began to the dull boom of the drums, and the dancers started into the circle, men and women in two lines, bells jangling on buckskin, and moccasins scuffing on dry earth. Mom and many of the younger women looked awkward and self-conscious, but Aunt Loretta and the older women moved confidently, even in their arthritic shuffling. At the foot of the dance pole, the Kiowa shaman began making his medicine.

The circle turned round, and I caught sight of Aunt Loretta again. She was smiling, her milky gaze fixed high on the cedar pole, and I imagined that she was seeing the medicine lifting with the beat of the drums and the rhythm of the chant, a spiral like smoke rising toward Heaven.

I looked again at Mom, saw that her eyes were

closed now and her feet certain in the dance. The beat drew me, pulled me a step toward the big drum where John Redwing chanted. But, then, beyond the pole, I saw Jim sitting on the rise in the shadow of the tribal center. And something about how he sat looking down on us held me back for the instant before I blinked and saw the picture clear again: a bunch of Indians beating drums and shuffling in the dust while an old man sang to himself in the center of the ring — sang words that perhaps even he no longer understood — and all the while, the white tourists recorded the scene with their video cameras, a scene that they might someday show bored grandkids of times past.

It took nearly an hour to make the medicine for rain. Then the rhythm of the drums changed, and the circle broke open, the older men and women moving to the side to rest, while the younger ones held out arms for the little kids waiting on the edge of the circle. A few plucky tourists tried to join the dance, as if it were some Hawaiian luau, and had to be shown out of the ring by the constables. Chuck let go of Heidi and Christine, and they ran to join Mom. She began showing them the steps, while Aunt Loretta and the other old women cackled and called out advice.

I went to stand by Chuck. "Hi," he said. "Going to take your turn?"

"You first."

"I think they'd spot me. Want to go get something cold?"

111

I glanced at the rise where Jim still sat. "Thanks, but I think I'll go talk to Jim for a while."

"Going to ride with us? Your mom's going to want to get the kids home around supper time."

"I'll get Jim to give me a ride. Or maybe I'll sleep over at his place."

"Okay," he said. "Be careful."

"Sure," I said.

I walked up the rise to where Jim sat in the lengthening shadow of the tribal center. "Hi," I said.

"Hi."

I sat on the dry grass next to him. "What'd you think?"

"I guess people enjoyed it, but I hope they're not counting on anything happening. No Kiowa shaman is gonna understand the situation around here."

"He's supposed to make it rain. No rain is no rain, whether it's here or Oklahoma."

"Yeah, but why hasn't there been any rain?"

"I don't know. The weatherman on channel nine says the jet stream is off course."

"And what's the shaman supposed to do about that?"

I lay back, staring at the hot sky. "Beats me."

"Then you don't believe in the medicine?"

"You know I don't."

He grunted. "Well, I do. Trouble is, I don't think he went after the right problem."

"And what's that?"

112

"That's what I've been trying to figure out."

"It's the jet stream," I said. "Pure and simple. And there isn't a damned thing anybody can do about it."

He didn't say anything for a long minute. "Maybe. Come on, let's go see if the party's started."

Main Street had become a carnival by the time we got there. Sweating tourists stood in line to buy pop, beer, ice cream, corn soup, and squaw-burgers at stands set up along the street. On the sidewalks, reservation folk had spread blankets and laid out baskets, jewelry, and leather work — almost all of it crap bought from wholesalers. Triple and his buddies were trying to eat themselves to death, and Harney had a thick wad of bills folded in his palm as he posed for yet another picture with smiling white kids.

Kim Halfaday was working one of the stands, selling bratwurst and fry bread to a long line of tourists. Jim sidled in beside her. "Need a couple of Blues and a Dew, Kimmy."

"Take my place for half an hour and I'll buy."

"Sorry, I'm not that thirsty."

"Too bad. Help yourself, then. Four bucks total."

"No discount?"

"Ha. Just get your beer; you're in the way."

Jim dug into the tub of ice for the cans, left four wrinkled dollar bills, and came back to where I was standing in the shadow of the alley, watching the crowd milling in the street. He handed me my pop, opened one of the beers, and drained it in three long swallows. He grunted and belched. "That's better." He opened the second beer and leaned against the side of the building, studying the street. "Amazing," he said. "Seven miles from here, the whole damned forest is getting ready to explode, and we throw a party for the tourists."

"Well, it was supposed to be serious."

"Yeah, for maybe ten percent of us. The rest are just out for the bucks."

We didn't talk much for maybe ten minutes. Finally, Jim crushed his empty can. "Well, I've had it with standing around here. Guess I'll drive up to Eddy's. Maybe borrow a boat from him and do a little fishing. Want to come along?"

"No, thanks," I said, knowing that he'd never get a boat or a line in the water.

Just then, Hal Strawback, Kim's boyfriend, squeezed through the crush of tourists and took shelter in the alley. "Hi," he said. "Thought you guys would be up at Billy Twodeer's."

"What's happening there?" Jim asked.

"Got a keg and some charcoal going."

"Hadn't heard," Jim said.

"Well, so much for the Indian telegraph. Kim's pissed as hell that she can't go, but I'm going anyway."

"How's your old man doing?" I asked.

Hal laughed. "Pa? Now there's somebody who's pissed. Committee agrees that this is going to be

114

a serious day, and then half of 'em run home to start making squawburgers to sell to the tourists. Pa and a couple of the others were so disgusted that they decided to get out of town right after the rain dance. They asked that shaman to go out in the woods with 'em to do a sweat bath. But he says, 'You, boys, go ahead; I've got a date.' Turns out that he's real friendly, and I mean *real* friendly, with Hannah Twodeer. So while the shaman and old lady Twodeer are off somewhere getting laid, Billy and Sonia are throwing a party." He laughed. "Shit. And the committee paid that shaman some good bucks, too. Some medicine man." I grinned, but Jim grimaced. "So, what do you say, guys? Want to head on up?"

"Sounds good to me," I said.

"Yeah, I guess," Jim said.

We rode in Jim's heap out beyond the edge of town to the Twodeers' frame house. There were maybe thirty kids already there, drinking beer and roasting hot dogs on the charcoal. The beer was mostly foam, and Jim stared at his glass in disgust: "Shit. You'd think after a couple of centuries, Indians would know how to tap a keg of beer." He drained his glass. "I've got to do something about this." He headed back to the keg.

I drifted around, talking to kids I hadn't seen since school let out in the spring. I kept a wary eye out for Mona, but didn't see her. Out in the woods, beyond the tribal center, a drum started to beat. The kids lifted their heads to listen. "I'll hand it to Pa," Hal said. "He doesn't quit. He and a couple of his buddies are even talking about trying to organize a chapter of the *midéwiwin* society. God, that's just what we need."

I didn't really know much about the old-time medicine lodge that had pretty much disappeared on this reservation way, way back. "I think we'd be better off with a vocational school and some jobs," I said.

"You got that right," Hal said. "Most of this old stuff is bullshit, if you ask me. What I want is a decent job once I graduate. But right now, I need another glass of this foam. Want one?"

"No, thanks."

Arms encircled me from behind, and I felt breasts press against my back. "Gotcha," Mona said. I turned. Her face was flushed and her eyes a little glassy. She grinned. "You still mad at me?"

"I'm not mad at you, Mona."

"Good. Come on, there's something I want to show you." She started pulling me toward the house.

"What is it?"

"You'll see."

I didn't want to make a scene, so I let her drag me into the house. I hesitated at the stairs to the upper floor. "Come on, scaredy," she said. "I ain't gonna bite you."

At the top of the stairs, she led me to Sonia's hot little room under the eaves. Through the window, we could hear kids laughing below in the yard and the steady beat of the drum in the distance. She drew me over to Sonia's littered desk. "Look, Sonia's got the pictures of when we went to Ashland." She flipped to the last pages of the album. I leaned over. There we were: posing in front of the fancy Winnebago camper, then on the main street, and still later on the beach, the gray waters of the lake behind us. The pictures were fuzzy, and I couldn't quite focus on them through the dull throb of my headache beating in time to the distant thud of the drum. I heard Mona close the door and looked up. She was standing with her back to it, her lips a little parted. I met her too-bright eyes, knowing then that I was going to let it happen, and knowing her knowing of it. She reached behind her to lock the door, and came across the distance to me.

When it was done and done again, although it made me sad the second time, she dressed with her back to me. She leaned over and kissed me softly. Tears sparkled in her deep brown eyes, and I knew that what I'd felt hadn't been what she'd wanted or hoped for, and that she'd known. She left without saying anything, and I dressed.

I left by the back door. Jim's car was gone, so I made my way across the field to the dirt road. Beyond the trees, the drum shuddered and fell silent, and I walked alone in the buzzing heat and the red dust toward town.

The carnival along Main Street was winding down as dusk came on and the tourists piled the last of their souvenirs and wedged their grease-filled bellies into their cars. An hour to an air-conditioned motel, and they could relax with a cold drink and the kids in the pool to tell humorous stories of the local wildlife.

Kim was packing up her stand, her motions impatient. "Party still going on?" she asked.

"Yeah," I said. "It's doing okay."

"Want a bratwurst? They're free."

I hadn't eaten since breakfast and was suddenly aware of the hollow in my stomach. "Thanks," I said.

"Help yourself to a soda, too. Hal staying out of trouble?"

"As far as I know."

"Good. Just as long as that little bitch Mona —" Her hands paused, and she looked up at me. "Hey, I'm sorry. I forgot."

"It's okay," I said. "Don't worry; they weren't together."

"That's good." She busied herself with boxing up the ketchup and mustard.

"Did you see Jim Redwing come by?" I asked.

"Yeah, I saw his car turn up toward the school about an hour ago. I thought you were with him."

"No. He took off while I wasn't looking. How about my folks?"

"Nope, haven't seen them. No, wait a second, I did, too. I saw them heading out about quarter after five, maybe five-thirty. Your sisters sure looked cute in their outfits."

"Yeah, they did. Well, thanks, Kim."

"Sure," she said. I'd started away when she said, "Say, I heard that you had trouble out your way."

"Not that I know of. What kind of trouble?"

"Some of the men were talking about some dog or wolf or something that got out of its cage."

"Yeah," I said. "Old white guy named Wilson has a dog he claims is part wolf. Wilson disappeared, and somebody let it out. Haven't heard of any trouble, though."

"Well, these guys were saying that it's been hanging around a couple of places over on the west side of the rez. One of them said that he had some chickens killed, and another said that he'd found a fawn killed by something big."

"A lot of things kill chickens and fawns."

"Guess so," she said, pitching a couple of serving spoons into a box. "There, to hell with this. I'm gonna go find Hal before he gets in trouble."

"Okay," I said. "We'll see you."

I wandered up the side street leading to the school, but Jim's car was nowhere in sight. Crap, I was going to have to hitchhike. I headed south along the road leading to the highway. I didn't expect any trouble getting a ride with a Chippewa family to the edge of the rez, but it'd get tough after that. I was maybe a quarter mile out of town, when I saw a car coming from the south. Its single headlight picked me out and then it swerved onto the shoulder, nearly went in the ditch, and skidded to a stop. Jim. I jogged to the car.

He was drunk, his words slurred. "Hey, *niijii*. What you doin' out here?"

"Trying to catch a ride home. Where you been?"

"Went over to Jack Royta's to smoke a little weed. I looked for you before I left Billy's but didn't see you and figured you'd gone someplace with Mona. Thought I'd get back, but, I don't know, shit got complicated."

"Move over," I said. "I'm driving."

"Be my guest." He slumped against the opposite door while I got the heap in gear. "Hey," he said, "let's go up to Eddy's."

"You don't need to go to Eddy's." I swung the car onto the pavement and headed north toward town.

"Yeah, I do. Maybe old man Wilson's up there just waitin' ta buy some hootch for this thirsty Chippewa boy."

"Not likely. I think he's long gone."

"Well, somebody'll be up there. . . . You got any money?"

"No," I lied. "How about you just sober up, and I'll try to get us through town without getting picked up?"

"Nobody picks up this car. This is a good Indian car."

"Right," I said, slowing as we rolled into town.

On the far side, I picked up speed again, and glanced over at Jim. His eyes were closed, and he was humming to himself. "Don't fall asleep," I said. "I don't want to carry you into the house."

"Hey, don't take me home, man. My uncle's there, and he'll give me hell again."

Maybe you ought to goddamn listen to him, I thought. "Where then? And don't say Eddy's. I don't think we've even got the gas to get there."

"Park up near the old chapel. No one's gonna bother us there."

"Okay," I said.

A mile north of the junction, I started watching for the rutted track that led to the abandoned mission church built by some nearly forgotten preacher who'd hoped to bring the heathen Chippewa to Jesus. A dark shape rocketed out of the ditch and shot across the road in front of us. I slammed on the brakes, feeling my foot go nearly to the floor as the heap bucked and slewed. Jim was thrown forward, somehow managing to catch himself before he hit the dashboard. I wrenched the wheel to the right to keep from sliding ass-end into the ditch and brought the heap to a shuddering stop.

"Holy shit," Jim said. "Did you see that thing?" He was sitting bolt upright, scared nearly sober.

I got my breath back. "Yeah," I said. "It was old man Wilson's mutt."

"Maybe it was tonight, man, but that ain't no

dog and it ain't no dogwolf. That goddamn thing's a shape-shifter. My granddad told me about them."

I laughed. "Come on. You never believed that garbage." He didn't say anything, but reached under the seat as I got the heap going again. His hand came out with a half-empty pint of whiskey. He opened it and took a long swallow. "Put that away," I said. "You don't need any more booze."

"The hell I don't," he said. "Remember that day we stopped to use the pump at Wilson's and I walked over to the cage? That beast growled and started to shift, man. I saw it."

"Started to shift into what?"

"I don't know," he said. "And I don't want to."

He took another swallow and offered the bottle to me. "No, thanks," I said. "I might start seeing things, too."

"Or at least start admitting it."

"Shut up," I said, "or I'll get out and leave you here by yourself."

"Yeah, you do that. I'd like to see you walk home in the dark with that goddamn thing out there somewhere."

We rode in an angry silence. I spotted the overgrown road leading to the chapel and slowed for the turn. We bumped down the road a few hundred yards, the long grass scraping against the undercarriage until I caught sight of the sagging roof of the chapel. I shut off the engine and the headlight, but left the dome light burning while I turned around to clear a place on the backseat. "I thought you were going to walk home," Jim said sarcastically.

"Too far," I said. I climbed into the backseat and stretched out.

Jim lay down in the front. "Shall I turn off the dome light or do you need a night-light?"

"Screw you," I said. "Go to sleep."

CHAPTER
SIX

I slapped myself awake at dawn trying to kill a mosquito buzzing around my ear. It was hot in the car, the air sour. I leaned over the front seat to check on Jim, but he wasn't there. I crawled out and stood for a minute, taking in lungfuls of fresh air and stretching the kinks out of my back and legs. The birds were singing in the cool of early morning, and I could see swallows flitting in and out from under the eaves of the old chapel. I walked down the path to it, tested the rickety steps, and climbed up to look through the doorway. People had come long since to take anything usable, leaving the inside bare except for a scattering of trash and the weeds pushing up through the rotten floor. The walls sagged inward, their strength all but exhausted under the weight of the roof and a dead preacher's dreams.

I'd heard from Aunt Loretta of how he'd come, way back during the Depression, which had hardly seemed worse to the Chippewa than ordinary times: "He was all filled with the golly-gollies for his Jesus and the love of his Chippewa brothers and sisters. He was a good man, you could see that, but a fool. He wanted us to come to his church and get baptized in the creek out behind. He said we'd be washed free of sin, although when we asked which sins, he'd blush and get too embarrassed to talk about them. He'd just say sins of the flesh, sins of the spirit. And we'd say: 'But what sins of the flesh do you mean,' not wanting to embarrass him more by asking about the other, because what could he know of an *Anishinaabe*'s sins of the spirit? And he'd mumble about adultery and lust and greed and a few of the others, and we'd say: 'But these are the same sins Father Shannon has been warning us about for years. What can you do about our sins that Father Shannon cannot?' And that stumped him, maybe because he did not know, or maybe because he didn't want to make an enemy of Father Shannon by telling us that it was no good being Catholic.

"We didn't make any more fun of him after that, and a few of the people even went to his chapel to hear him preach, because we all knew he was a good man and we wanted to be polite. But it was a long way to go, because not many *Anishinaabe* had cars back then. And, besides, if you went more than a time or two, he'd start talking about washing away sins, and no one wanted to get dunked in that cold creek. So, after a while, no one bothered to go anymore. He lived alone in his chapel all winter, eating I don't know what, since he'd spent the few dollars he had at the trading post that fall.

"Finally, Jamie Lonetree came into town with news that the preacher was dying. Old Father Shannon got on his coat and took his black case packed with the sacraments. Jamie and a couple of the other men rode along in Father's old Model-A. They had to walk the last half mile on snow-shoes, dragging a sledge behind them. Father went into the chapel, and came out a while later to tell the men that it was no good trying to pull the preacher out on the sledge because he was dying for sure. He told them to go home, but Jamie and the others talked and decided that if Father Shannon could wait, so could they. They built a fire and squatted by it, because they didn't want to get too close to the place of death. And they waited through the night, listening to the wind and the cold, while Father sat with that strange young man until death slipped in and took his spirit away.

"In the morning, Father Shannon wrapped the body in a blanket and told Jamie and the others to dig a grave. But the ground was frozen deep, even under the place where they'd built the fire, and they told Father Shannon that it could not be done. So Father tied the body to a board, and together they wedged it over the rafters of that little chapel and left it there. Later, when the story got around, some of the people disapproved, say-ing that the preacher's ghost would always haunt the place after that. The talk of ghosts made Father angry, and he was very stern with the people that winter. In the spring, he went out there and dug the grave himself and came back into town all dirty with the digging and looking very sad. After that, he never spoke of the preacher again, and neither did any of us in Father's presence. Besides, what was there to say? He'd been a good man, but a fool."

I stepped off the rotted porch and walked into the woods. Jim was sitting on the bank of the stream where the preacher had planned to wash away the sins of a Chippewa flock that had never come. The drought had narrowed the stream to a sludgy rivulet, but I was too sticky with sweat and sleep to care. I stretched out on my belly and splashed a double handful of water on my face and then rinsed my mouth. I sat back and looked at Jim, noticing the empty whiskey bottle lying a few feet away. "How's the head?" I asked.

"Not too bad yet. It'll be worse later."

I grunted and looked at the growing light. "I have to get going pretty quick," I said. "I've got to be in the tower by seven."

"Take a minute to walk upstream. Go about a hundred paces until you come to a clump of balsams, then cut to your right for another thirty yards or so. Look for a forked maple."

"What's there?"

"You'll see."

I went, finding the balsams without trouble and cutting into the hardwoods like he'd said. The skull was gray-green with age, wedged like a rotten fungus in the fork of an old maple. I went close to study the heavy jaw, the long teeth, and the vacant eye sockets beneath the low forehead. Bear.

Jim didn't look at me when I sat down next to him again. "Find it?"

"Yeah. Some hunter got a bear and tried to keep the head off the ground and away from the animals until he could come back for it. Never got around to it, I guess."

"Maybe. Or maybe the last Bear cult put it there. They used to put them in trees, decorate them with ribbons, and pray for the spirit of Bear to protect them."

"No ribbons on it now."

"No. Not anymore." He still didn't look at me.

"How long have you known about it?"

"Couple of years."

"Why didn't you ever mention it?"

"Didn't mean anything to me then."

"And it does now?"

"Maybe."

"What?"

"I'm thinking about that. . . . Hey, you'd better get going. Just leave the heap on that old logging road northeast of the tower."

"That's five miles," I said. "Sure you want to walk that far?"

"I know a shortcut. Besides, I don't have anything else to do." He stared at the stream. "Not much water left," he said. "Hardly enough to dunk a decent-sized Indian even if you had a preacher."

"Probably not. You sure you want to walk?"

"Yeah, go ahead. Put the keys behind the visor or just leave them in the ignition. Nobody's gonna steal that car, anyway."

"Okay," I said. "You take care, huh?"

"Sure," he said.

I parked the heap near the mouth of the logging road and walked the rest of the way, skirting the swamp around the rocky island where the three tall pines grew, and then cutting southwest until I saw the tower loom through a break in the hardwoods. I climbed up and turned on the radio in time to hear Steve begin to sign in the towers. I answered when it was my turn and then made coffee while he gave the morning briefing: two new fires overnight, both under control now; temperatures in the high nineties with a chance of thunderstorms late; fire danger extreme; don't anybody be a hero if the big one comes your way.

When there didn't seem to be any more radio traffic, I keyed the handset. "Crescent Lake, this is One-One."

"This is Crescent Lake. Go ahead, One-One."

"Steve, when you get a chance, will you pick up the phone and give my mom a call? Tell her I'm okay. That I camped out with Jim last night."

Another voice came in. "Uh, Crescent Lake, suspect One-One's transmission is bogus. Request clarification on the sex of the camping companion."

There were a couple of chortles from other stations and a "Who's the main squeeze, One-One? We need details."

Steve interrupted. "All stations, cool it. This is a working circuit, remember? One-One, Roger. I'll give her a ring."

I thanked him and leaned back in my chair, studying the dull cloud over the forest. No Kiowa rain clouds on the horizon, no change at all. Just heat and smoke and the end of the world if the big one breached our line.

I walked home by way of old man Wilson's, no longer bothering to pause at the edge of the clearing to check for signs of life. And maybe that's why the sight of the cabin door hanging open hit me with a jolt that nearly made me pee my pants. I jumped back into the shadow of the shed across the way. The silence hung like something waiting, and for a long minute, I couldn't pull my eyes away from the yawning darkness beyond the door. I forced myself to study the yard. There were tire tracks in the dust of the driveway, how old I couldn't guess, but whoever had driven in slowly had left in a hurry, gouging the earth with spinning tires on his way out.

I waited ten minutes, the thudding of my heart the only sound in the silence. Get a grip, I told myself. Wilson came home and left again. Or maybe somebody dropped him off, and he's lying in there on his bed, too drunk to close the door.

Or maybe somebody broke in to see what they could rip off. But there ain't anything in there that's going to eat you. Now just slide around the corner and get the hell out of here. Tell Chuck about it later and let him investigate.

But I had to know. So I took a breath, stepped out of the shadows, and crossed the yard, the sound of my boots on the dry earth suddenly very loud. The porch creaked under my weight, and I hesitated, listening for a snore, a movement, any sound inside. Nothing, just the humming of insects in the woods and the thudding of my own heart. I stepped into the shadow of the door, waited again, and then cautiously peeked around the side.

It took my eyes a minute to adjust to the gloom of the cabin. The bed was empty, the room seemingly undisturbed from its usual state of disorder. Three guns still hung on a rack on the wall, a fairly new Coleman lantern stood in a corner, and a half a dozen usable tools lay on the table near the door. I started to take a step inside, but stopped dead when I saw what was written in yellow soap on the mirror over the old dresser: "You got it coming, you bastards!" Shaking, I backed off the porch, turned, and ran.

After supper, I asked Chuck to come outside. I told him what I'd found and what was written on the mirror. He frowned. "Did Wilson come back?"

"I don't know," I said. "Maybe."

"Nothing was taken?"

"Not that I could tell. There were three guns in the rack on the wall."

"Nobody breaks into a place and leaves guns behind. Not in this country. I'm going to call the sheriff."

He came out of the house five minutes later. "There's been a big accident south of Ashland. Tanker truck and a couple of cars. They said they'd get somebody out here in the morning."

I hesitated, not wanting to volunteer. "Should we go lock up the place?"

"No, they said leave everything the way it is." He stood staring at the spot where the road disappeared into the trees on its way to Wilson's. He shook his head violently, as if to chase an unwanted thought.

"What?" I asked.

"Oh, nothing. I just can't figure out that message. It's like he turned that damned dogwolf loose himself and was giving us a warning."

"That doesn't figure," I said. "The place was all locked up when I found the dogwolf gone. I don't think Wilson had been around at all."

"Yeah, I know. It was just a silly thought. Well, I'll probably be gone by the time a deputy gets here. Tell him what you know."

"Sure," I said.

The girls were finishing breakfast, and Mom and I were sitting on the back steps having a second

132

cup of coffee when a deputy sheriff's car pulled into the yard. Mom craned her neck to get a look at the driver. "It's Bert Weathers," she said. "I went to high school with him."

"Looks like it," I said, feeling my stomach tighten. Crazy Horse.

He grinned when he saw Mom, the hardness disappearing from his heavy, pockmarked face. "Hi, Jan. Been some time."

"Sure has, Bert. Making good?"

"Oh, yeah. This affirmative action stuff is great. Another ten years and they'll let me sit in the office once a month."

"Oh, you'd be bored in the office. Bert, this is my boy, Pete."

"Sure, I've seen him around." He stuck out a huge hand. I took it, feeling the power as it folded around mine. "Sticking to the back roads?" he asked.

"Uh, yeah. Sure."

"Good," he said. "That's good." He let my hand go, the knowing in his eyes making me shift uncomfortably.

"Cup of coffee?" Mom asked.

"That'd be great if you've got some made."

"Just a minute."

She got up and went into the kitchen. I heard Heidi ask, "Can we play in the police car?"

"Yeah, that'd be neat," Christine said.

Mom said, "Not on your life. Finish your breakfast and put the dishes in the sink."

Bert grinned. "I'll turn on the siren for them."
He glanced around, spotted a lawn chair, and
pulled it over to the steps. He sat and put his
clipboard on his knee. "So, what've we got here?
Old man Wilson's been gone a while, and now
someone's broken into his place."

"Well, I'm not sure. He might have come back
and then left again." I told him what I knew.

Mom came back out with his cup of coffee, and
he sipped at it while he wrote. "Nothing taken,
then?"

"Not that I could tell."

"Guns still hanging on the wall, you said?"

"Yeah. A .22, a double-barreled 12-gauge, and
an old model nine-four .30-30. The full-length
model with the octagon barrel."

"Hmm. That's worth two or three hundred. Very
strange." We heard the sound of a car pulling into
the drive. Bert turned in his seat. "Not much of a
muffler on that one." Jim drove into the yard. "Ah,
young Master Redwing," he said, and I thought:
Oh, shit.

Mom hesitated, and then said, "He's a friend of
Pete's." Bert grunted.

At the sight of Bert's squad, Jim would suddenly
want to be somewhere else, but it was too late to
get out of it now. He parked and walked across
the yard, trying not to look self-conscious. He was
sober, thank God, but he looked tired and drawn.
"Hi," he said. "Thought I'd see if you had the coffee
pot on."

Mom smiled. "Sure." She went into the house again.

Bert had turned back to his clipboard. He asked without looking up, "Keeping it out of the ditch this week, Redwing?"

"Yes, sir. Been straight as an arrow."

"Good. Keep it that way." He finished writing and looked at me. "Get your sisters, and I'll let them turn on the siren."

Jim stood beside me as the three of them went off to the squad, the girls dancing with excitement. Passing Jim's car, Bert slowed for a look inside. "I hope to hell you don't have an uncased gun in there," I said quietly.

"It's in the trunk," Jim whispered. "We've got to talk."

"About what?"

Mom came out the door then and handed Jim a cup of coffee. "Sorry it took so long, Jim. I had to make you instant."

"Thanks," he said.

We watched while the girls tried out the siren and then spent a minute wrestling with the locked steering wheel and making driving sounds. Then Bert said that was enough and brought them back. He looked at Jim and me. "Well, let's go have a look."

Jim rode in the back behind the cage separating the seats. Bert glanced in his rearview mirror. "At home back there, Redwing?" Jim gave a sickly grin, and Bert smiled slightly.

Bert parked a couple of hundred feet up the road from Wilson's, picked up a Polaroid camera from the seat beside him, and we walked down. He paused to study the tire tracks in the yard. "Somebody left in a hurry, that's for sure." He walked over to the cabin and stepped inside. I followed, while Jim stayed in the doorway. I sensed it immediately: something had changed. I looked around, trying to spot it. The guns were still hanging on the rack, but I thought a couple of the drawers in the dresser might have been pulled out and not pushed back all the way. I glanced down and saw the track of a boot with a lynx-paw sole in the dust by the table. Jim saw it, too, and I felt him tense. As casually as I could, I shifted a foot over the print and scuffed it out.

Bert was studying the message scrawled on the mirror. "Would either of you recognize Wilson's handwriting?"

"Not me," I said. Jim shook his head.

Bert grunted and spent a couple of minutes poking around. "Well, let me get some pictures, and then we'll lock up."

He shot the pictures while we waited out in the yard. "When were you here, Jim?" I said quietly.

"Wait until he's gone," Jim hissed.

Bert finished and locked the door behind him. He spent a minute scrawling a note on his pad, tore it out, and stuck it in the crack above the lock. "I'm going to leave a note telling Wilson to call us, but you call me if you see his truck come by.

From what I know of him, I doubt if he's going to be in any big hurry to call the department."

"Yes, sir," I said.

He paused by the open door of the cage. "I heard he had one hell of a mean dog here. Half wolf or something. What happened to it?"

"I don't know," I said. "I was feeding it for a while, but it was gone when I came by a few days ago."

"Think Wilson let it out?"

"I kind of doubt it. I didn't see any sign that he'd been around. . . . Is it okay if Jim and I walk back now?"

"Fine with me. Stay out of trouble."

We said "Yes, sir" and started into the woods while he took a picture of the tire tracks. When we were safely out of earshot, Jim said, "God, that guy's a hard-ass."

I didn't let him dodge. "When did you come by, Jim? Did you break in a couple of days ago?"

He shook his head. "Not me. I came by this morning just after dawn and saw the door open."

"And you searched the place."

"Yeah, I had a look around."

"Why, Jim? What were you looking for?"

"I don't know. . . . I just wanted to see, that's all."

"See what?" He shrugged, and I got mad. "Damn it, Jim. If you were going to search the place, you should have been more careful. Leaving that track was dumb. Real dumb. Now what the hell were you looking for?"

He sighed. "Look, I've been out in the woods since you left me yesterday morning at the chapel. This morning I walked over to get my car, and . . . I don't know. I just decided to see if the dogwolf had come back. You know, been wandering around waiting for Wilson."

"And?"

"I think he has. There are some tracks and a patch of flattened grass over behind the shed like he'd been lying there watching. Maybe he scared off the people who broke in. Anyway, when I saw the door open, I went in and looked around."

"Why?"

He hesitated. "I thought maybe I could pick up a clue where Wilson got that beast and why he was keeping him."

"For God's sake, Jim, it was his dog. Why are you making things so complicated? Just because everybody else thought that creature was danger-ous doesn't mean that Wilson didn't like it."

"He hated it," Jim said. "You know he did."

"No, I don't," I said.

"Right," he said sarcastically. "Then suppose you tell me why he built that cage strong enough to hold a grizzly bear. And who gave him the money? Shit, that cage cost more than Wilson ever had. Somebody wanted that dog kept locked up, and Wilson got the job."

I stopped and looked at him. "You are out of your mind. Next you're going to start telling me that shape-shifter crap again. Come on, Jim. Either you've been drinking way too damned much, or the heat's making you *windigo*."

"All right," he said evenly. "I was drunk the other night, and maybe I said some stuff that didn't make any sense. All I'm saying now is that cage was built to keep something in until it died. You can call it a dog or a wolf or whatever you like. Me, I'm not sure what it is. But I do know the son of a bitch is loose now, and that scares the hell out of me."

We stood staring at each other. "Why did you spend the night in the woods?" I asked quietly.

"I don't know. Waiting for something, I guess."

"What?"

"I don't know. I wish to God I did."

Mom was hanging clothes when we got back to the farm. "They want you to sit tower this afternoon," she called. "Mac's got to take his wife to a doctor's appointment."

"Okay." I looked at Jim. "Want to come along?"

"No," he said. "I'm going home to take a shower. Uncle John will be on the road by now. Want me to run you over to the tower?"

"Yeah, that'd be good."

We rode in silence, both knowing that the other knew things that he wasn't telling about the dog-wolf. Mac saw us coming and was halfway down the ladder by the time we rolled into the clearing below the tower. As usual, he didn't stop to talk, just smiled, waved, and beat it. I told Jim thanks, got out, and started up the ladder.

I checked in with Steve, had a glance at the log-book, and then took my seat on the deck. I didn't want to be there, didn't want any extra time to think about Jim or Mona or Dad or why I'd been stupid enough to let the dogwolf out of his cage. But I was alone, and there was no avoiding the questions that had no answers — or answers that I couldn't even begin to guess.

Steve came on the radio early in the afternoon. "All stations, this is Crescent Lake. We've got a request from the sheriff's department for a scan of your sectors for a dark blue '81 Ford pickup. Give it a look, guys. Seems there's an old guy missing from down around One-One."

"This is One-Six. Who's the guy, One-One?"

I keyed the mike. "Guy named Wilson."

"Hein Wilson? Hell, I know him. He's just off someplace drunk. Or maybe in a whorehouse in Hurley."

"I thought they cleaned up Hurley," another voice said.

A couple of other tower jockeys immediately offered opinions on the health of organized sin in Hurley. Steve broke in. "This is Crescent Lake. For God's sake, guys, shut up. How many times do I have to tell you? We've got a job to do, and we've got to keep the circuit clear for business traffic." Someone gave a Bronx cheer, but the chatter stopped.

I already knew every foot of the surrounding couple of miles, but I did a slow circuit of the deck to inspect the woods for any glint of unexpected blue showing through the trees. Nothing.

The day dragged on, nobody reporting anything. The spotter plane flew lazy circles over the forest, the sound of its engine coming faintly across the distance. A hot wind came up in the west, rippling the branches of the trees and thickening the harsh smell of burning peat. It was nearly four when a voice came on the radio. "Crescent Lake, this is One-Four. I just picked up the smallest bit of blue bearing two-one-seven, range about fifteen hundred yards. Can't tell if it's a car or what."

"Roger, One-Four. We'll send Air Spot in for a look."

I watched as the plane swept in over the northeastern corner of Chuck's sector. The plane circled for ten minutes, then took on altitude. Steve came back on. "Air Spot confirms blue pickup. Good work, One-Four. You other guys call in anything you see. There are a lot of blue pickups in the world."

Chuck set down his knife and fork and leaned back. "They sent in a ground unit for a look. It was old man Wilson's pickup all right. The boys looked around for him, but there's a lot of territory out there." He glanced at me. Yeah, a lot of territory — the same territory where my father had gone to die.

"What do you suppose he was doing up there?" Mom asked.

"Hell, I don't know. His brain was probably so pickled by the time he got off his bender that he thought he was on the road home. Anyway, the sheriff asked for help putting the search party together, and guess who got stuck with that?"

"You did," Heidi yelped.

Christine started crying. "I was going to say that. How come she always gets to guess first?"

"Because she's a blabbermouth," Mom said, pulling Christine onto her lap. "Now hush your crying and let Daddy finish."

Heidi was pouting, and Chuck made a place for her on his lap. "I can't pull more than a few guys off the fire crews, so I'll have to get bodies somewhere else. What do you say, Pete? Want to beat the brush for the old fool?"

"I wouldn't mind, but I've got to sit tower tomorrow."

"Call Mac; he'll take your day. Think you and your buddy Jim could round up a few of your friends?"

"I suppose. What's it going to pay?"

"Minimum wage. We'll get some coffee and doughnuts out there in the morning, but people should bring a sandwich and something to drink. We'll start at six and knock off at six if we don't find anything. Then we'll keep doing it until somebody tells us to quit."

I glanced at the clock. "I'd better get going if I'm going to find anybody."

"Drive careful," he said.

*   *   *

Jim was home for a change, sitting on the worn sofa in his underwear, watching TV. He gestured with the beer can in his hand. "Want a Blue?"

"No, thanks." I explained about the search party. "So do you want to go?"

Jim stared at the can in his hand. "Might as well, I guess. I kinda figured it'd come to this." He crushed the can and tossed it in the general direction of a wastebasket. "Let's go see who's around."

We had pretty good luck, recruiting a dozen kids, including Hal, Kim, Billy, and Sonia. Sonia said she'd get in touch with Mona, and I couldn't think of a good reason to tell her not to.

Overnight, the Indian telegraph spread the word, and about thirty Chippewa were at the Forest Service headquarters at six the next morning. With a couple of sheriff's deputies and the half dozen guys Chuck had pulled from the fire crews, there was quite a crowd munching doughnuts, slurping coffee, and gossiping by the time Chuck climbed onto the bed of a pickup to get everybody settled down. He let Bert Weathers do the briefing: "Okay, people. We're looking for a guy named Heinrich Wilson, a white Caucasian about sixty-five years old, give or take. He's also known as Henry, Hank, and to the few people who ever gave a damn, as Hein. As far as we know, nobody's seen him in about a week, although we think his truck's only been here three or four days. We're going to sweep an area from east to west between the fire lane where we found his pickup and . . ." He turned to check the map Chuck was holding. Chuck put a finger on a spot, and they talked quietly for a moment. "Okay. Between fire lane four-one-seven and Two Pine Creek. That's a distance of roughly three miles. There's another fire lane, four-one-nine, on the far side of the creek. If we don't find him in the first sweep, we'll regroup there, count heads, and then sweep an area to the north. Everybody's going to get their feet a little wet crossing the creek, but there isn't anything we can do about that. Now for God's sake, people, don't anybody get lost. Stay in sight of the person on either side of you and don't get too far ahead and don't lag behind."

Behind me, Mona said, "Aw, shucks. I was counting on a little lagging behind." Sonia giggled.

Bert had another quick conversation with Chuck and then continued, his face grim. "Now we're not expecting anything good out of this, people. Chances are he's dead somewhere out there. If you find him alive or if you find him dead, don't move him. Just give a holler, and Chuck, Deputy Greenwald, and I will be there in a few minutes. We'll have radios and we'll know what to do. Any questions?"

No one had any, and we piled into the Forest Service pickups for the ride through the woods to the fire lane where One-Four had spotted Wilson's truck. At the jump-off point, there was a good deal of milling around until Chuck and the deputies got everybody in a line. I was relieved when Mona got stuck near the center, and Jim and I were given places toward the northern end. At a signal from Bert, we started into the brush. It was heavy going in the heat, the word coming down the line every couple of hundred yards to hold up for stragglers. We were scraped up by blackberry brambles and half chewed to death by mosquitoes by the time we stumbled across Two Pine Creek at midmorning and found the fire lane a hundred yards beyond.

People came out of the woods in twos and threes, pulling burrs from their clothing and checking for wood ticks. Bert and the other deputy looked disgusted, and Chuck looked older than I could ever remember. He leaned against one of the Forest Service trucks brought around from the jump-off, his face pale beneath the tan. I walked over to him. "How's it going?"

"I'm not as young as I used to be, that's for sure."

"Can't be as tough as fighting fires."

"I guess not. Just feeling off my stuff today."

"Maybe you ought to stay with the trucks this time."

"No, I'm okay. Go get something to drink." He waved me toward another truck, where people were getting cups of lemonade.

"I'll bring you one."

"Yeah, do that."

After half an hour, they got us in line again, and we started back to the east, covering the area north of our first sweep. We'd gone maybe a half mile when there was a shout to our left. "They've found something," Jim said. "Let's go."

Pushing through the brush toward the shouting, we broke through a thicket into a little clearing and saw him hanging there from the lowest branch of a big pine; saw what the crows had done to him, how they'd taken his tongue and his eyes and pulled his brains out through the eye sockets so that gray strands hung dried on his cheeks; saw how the heat had bloated him, popped the buttons on his shirt, split his pants, and turned his skin black; and saw then that we'd been wrong, that his skin was still white beneath the cloud of flies that rose from him, borne upward on a stench that must have turned the stomachs of the sky people had they come down on wings to see what we had seen. I was sick then, down on my hands and knees, crying between feeling my stomach empty and empty again, feeling Jim down on one knee beside me, his hand resting on my back, as he stared at what was left of old man Wilson. And Jim started to chant, so softly that I could hardly hear the words, words of a death chant that I did not know how he could know or that I could know other than that we had been born knowing.

A lot of people were in the clearing when Jim helped me up. "Let's go; there's nothing we can do here," he said. I was still crying and could only nod.

Mona and Sonia came over, both trying not to

look at what hung from the tree. "Is he okay?" Mona asked in a small voice.

"Yeah, he's okay, Mona. It's just . . . Look, I'll tell you later. Or maybe Sonia knows about Pete's dad. I'm just going to get him out of here now. Tell Chuck he's with me and that we're going back home."

Mona hesitated. "We'll tell him," Sonia said.

We were nearly back to the cars before I could choke out: "Why? Why'd he do it?"

"I don't know," Jim said. "Things just connected up that way. After a while, everything connects. We just never know all the ways."

"Why'd you chant for him? He wasn't Chippewa."

"I didn't chant for him. I chanted for myself."

"A death chant?"

"Was that what it was? Hell, I just wanted to keep my mind off things. You puked, I chanted so that I wouldn't. It was the first song that came to mind."

"You're crazy," I said. "You shouldn't mess with that stuff."

"No, I guess not. . . . There's headquarters. Come on, I've got a bottle in the car."

"I couldn't," I said. "I'd get sick again."

"Well, I can," he said.

But at the car, Jim didn't get the bottle from under the seat. Instead, he spent a long moment gazing back into the forest where they'd be cutting old man Wilson down from the low branch of that big pine. Then he got in and cranked the starter until the heap finally started. I rode curled up against the far door, still sick and crying again. Jim seemed a million miles away, his right hand relaxed on the steering wheel and his eyes black slits against the hot wind and the smell of smoke blowing in through the open windows.

CHAPTER
SEVEN

I couldn't keep Jim's crazy ideas about the dogwolf out of my head, couldn't help wondering if Wilson had gone over the edge when he'd come back from his bender to find the cage door open and the dogwolf gone. "You got it coming, you bastards!" he'd written. What did I have coming? And when?

Bert Weathers came by to talk to Chuck and me. We couldn't tell him anything new, and he seemed to be going through the motions anyway. An old drunk had hung himself, no big deal.

Big Bill Caswell called a day later to ask if I'd seen anything of the dogwolf. He'd been getting complaints about a big something lurking around a campground north of the rez, knocking over garbage cans and scaring the tourists. He laughed. "Some said it was a big dog, some said it was a bear, and a couple of people even claimed that it was a wolf. A wolf! Can you believe that? Anyway, I thought I'd check to see if you'd seen Wilson's mutt."

"I haven't seen him, but somehow I don't think

that'd be his style. He just wouldn't hang around where there were a lot of people."

"Yeah, my bet's on a bear. But can you believe these tourists? A wolf, for God's sake. No self-respecting wolf would go within five miles of that place. Well, let me know if you see Wilson's dog. If you've got a gun handy, shoot it and save me the trouble."

I dreamed in fire that night, as I did almost every night in those days. Dreamed of fire and shifting shapes and a drum that shook me with its soundless beat. And when I came awake, sweating in my hot little room, the dreams stayed with me for a long time after I could make out the dim outline of my window against the night sky. I knew that in another time — or even now on a reservation where the *midéwiwin*, the old religion, still lived — that I might have been able to make some sense of my dreams, that I might have gone on a vision quest and come to know the meaning by going into the woods and waiting for some manito to pity me.

It had worked that way once. Or so I'd been told. The manito in the four layers of sky above or in the four layers of earth below would grant the Indian power, would grant it if the Indian came humbly, knowing his own weakness in a universe beyond full knowing. Manito that took shapes that Indians could understand: Bear, Otter, Thunderbird, Raven, Snake — and Wolf.

And those who had the courage to take the really

big risks, to call on power time and time again, became shamans: *tcisaki*, the tent-shakers, or *na-nandawi*, the healers, or *wabeno*, the men of the dawn sky, who could hold fire in their bare hands. And a few among those many, the few who could survive with power longest, came to know it so well that they became more spirit than human, became like manito themselves, shape-shifters no longer concerned with good and evil, but only with power itself.

But all that was crap. Old stuff practiced by illiterate savages. I didn't believe. Had never believed. Hell, I hadn't even learned it from some ancient teacher of little Chippewa children or even from chance bits and pieces overheard in the talk of old people. I'd learned it from a book while doing a paper for my history class in school: "B +, needs a stronger conclusion," Mrs. Barnes had written. God, didn't we all.

The girls came down with the flu, and Mom browbeat me into making the weekly visit to Aunt Loretta for her. I drove over to the rez. Aunt Loretta greeted me at the door, asked how the girls were feeling, and then led me into her living room.

I ate the cookies and drank the iced tea she gave me, and tried to think of something to say. Usually, the past was a foolproof subject, but that day she didn't seem much interested, dismissing my questions with an "oh, that was a long time ago" and a flick of her hand. I searched about in my head and then asked her what she remembered of the *midéwiwin*.

"Oh, you don't want to know about all that sorcery and witchcraft and stuff," she said. "The priests drove all that evil away. Father Shannon got very angry if he caught any of the people practicing the old way."

"Did he have a fight with the *midé*?"

She smiled, remembering. "When Father first came, an old *midé* shaman put a curse on him. He was Harney's uncle, although I don't think you'd get Harney to admit it now. Father heard, and he went straight to the old man's cabin. He didn't trade spells or prayers with the old man. No, he took him by the scruff of the neck and dragged him out into the street to show the people what a pathetic old fool that shaman was."

"So he didn't really have any powers?"

"Oh, perhaps he had a few, but Father's were greater. The people feared the old man, but they loved Father, even when he was strict with them, because they always knew that he loved them, while the old man was greedy only for money, power, and the young women."

"What became of the shaman after that?"

Aunt Loretta laughed her ancient, whispery laugh. "Why nothing. The people stopped fearing him, and every Sunday on his way to mass, Father would stop at the old man's door and call to him to drag his carcass out. He called him an 'old reprobate,' I remember that. And the old man would limp out on his crutch and follow Father down the street to the church like some crippled old dog, while the people laughed at him. Father was very hard on him for two years, never allowing him the sacrament because he did not think the old man had truly repented. Then finally the old man took sick and was going to die, and Father at last gave him the sacrament so that he could go in peace."

"And Father Shannon?"

"He was our priest until he was past seventy. He ministered to us and helped us get what was coming to us from the government. Finally, he had a stroke, and they took him away. A year or so later, they told us that Father had died in a home for retired priests. I don't think they'd ever paid him much, but he'd never spent much, either, and he left the church welfare fund seven thousand dollars in his will. It was his last gift to us.

"The new priest they gave us was a young man who smiled all the time and never won the people's respect. He started drinking with the men, trying to make friends. And when that didn't work, he just drank by himself until he was so crazy that they came and took him away. Some whispered that reading Father Shannon's diary drove him to drink, but I never believed that. It was just foolish talk, and he was just a whiskey priest. He used to come back sometimes when there was a dance, dressed just like ordinary folk. People would ask him if he was still a priest, and he'd smile like his stomach hurt and nod, but he'd never say much, and no one wanted to pry. So the people left him alone, and he'd stand off to the side, sad and lonely, watching the dancers as if he was expecting something. Since him, we've had many priests, many of them good men, but none like Father Shannon."

"But Aunt Loretta, even if you are a Catholic, you must believe in some of the old religion. I saw your face at the dance and you believed then."

She chuckled. "Believed in what? That we Chippewa are good people and that our prayers are heard by the Great Spirit? I believe that, and I believe that dancing is a form of prayer that comes easily to the *Anishinaabe*."

"But how about the Kiowa shaman?"

She gave a tiny shrug: "Perhaps he knew something that would make our prayers more attractive to the Great Spirit. Perhaps not. It was the dancing, the being together as a people, that made the difference." She leaned forward to touch my arm. "You think too much, Peter, make things too difficult when everything is really very simple."

"How?" I asked. "How is it so simple?"

"Because it's just life, that's all." She leaned back into the cushions of her chair. "That is an old lady's secret that you will have to learn on your own."

"When?" I asked.

"In time," she said. The hot wind blew in through the open windows, and she closed her eyes, the faint smile still on her lips.

I sat for a few minutes and then got up quietly.

I hesitated, then leaned over and touched her shoulder. "Aunt Loretta, I should be going."

She didn't open her eyes, only reached out to touch my arm with a wrinkled hand. "Go in beauty, Peter," she murmured in the old talk.

I walked downtown past Mona's, half tempted to knock on the door to see if she was home, but I couldn't think of what I'd say to her other than that I didn't want any talk, just some time between the sheets with her and a chance to forget everything else for a little while. But that wouldn't work, and I knew it.

Main Street lay nearly empty in the afternoon heat. Triple and his buddies sprawled in their hollows on the shady side of the trading post. Triple must have been feeling energetic, because he actually opened an eye to gaze at me for a second. Harney dozed, head on chest, in his rocking chair at the end of the porch. When the step creaked under my foot, he raised his head. "Sorry," I said. "Just a poor Chippewa boy."

He grunted. "Think I'll go on vacation. None of the tourists are. Get me a soda, scout. I'm dry."

"You buying?"

He grumbled and dug change out of a pocket. "No respect from the young. And to think I wasted good advice on you."

When I brought the sodas back, he grunted an ill-tempered thanks. "No tourists at all, huh?" I asked.

"Only one goddamn car all day. I think the warnings about the fire danger have started sinking in."

"Maybe so."

He rocked some. "One of the Forest Service boys was in town yesterday recruiting another fire team. They must be getting ready for the big one."

"They're pretty nervous. Chuck hasn't been home in three days except to take a shower and get fresh clothes."

Harney stopped rocking. "You know, scout, a big fire might be pretty good for business. Get some newspaper reporters in here. I'm a good interview."

"God, Harney, not even you could be that cynical."

He chuckled. "Maybe not, but I'm working on it. So how's it going, Pete?"

"Okay."

"You on that search party that found the old white guy hanging from a tree?"

"Yeah, I was there."

"He was the guy with the big wolfdog, right? Boy, has there been some talk about that creature."

My stomach tightened. "I hadn't heard."

"Better check your telegraph connection, scout. He's the big news. Seems that three nights ago he got into Phil Patch's chicken house. Killed a couple dozen of his leghorns. Phil took a shot at him with a 12-gauge when he was heading out. Thought he winged him, but couldn't have got him solid, because day before yesterday he was over at . . . Oh, hell, what's that gym teacher's name?"

"Ferguson," I said.

"Right, Ferguson. Well, you know, his wife's been trying to raise a dozen sheep up on their place off the North Fork road. That wolfdog comes roaring in there just about dusk. Tears into those sheep and kills three of 'em. Ferguson's collie takes out after him, and that wolfdog just cuts the shit out of him. Rips off one ear and half the other, takes out an eye, and does God knows what else to that poor dog before Ferguson's wife gets there and tries to hit the bastard with a shovel. Then the son of a bitch turns on her, and if she hadn't had enough sense to scream and run like hell, I think it would have done the same to her. Vet had to put down the collie. Too bad. It was a pretty good dog."

He looked up at me, expecting a comment. All I could manage was, "Yeah, I saw it a couple of times. Nice dog."

"Anyway, the whole thing's got people pretty stirred up. Too bad Patch isn't a better shot."

"Yeah," I said. "Hey, Harney, I gotta go. We'll see you."

"Sure. See any tourists, send 'em over."

I was so overwhelmed by Harney's news that I almost plowed right into Mona and Hal Strawback coming out of the youth center. They were holding hands and laughing. Hal saw me and reddened, but it didn't faze Mona. She grinned. "Hi, Petey boy. How you doin'?" I mumbled something about "fine," and she laughed at me. They kept going. I looked after them. She was swinging her hips, knowing that I'd be watching and wanting me to see what I was going to be missing. I made my feet move, not wanting anyone to see me feeling suddenly very alone on the sunlit street.

Driving home, I tried to figure out why it hurt so much. Somehow, knowing that Mona still wanted me, even when I'd treated her like crap, had connected me to reality like the voices on the radio during the long days I sat alone in the tower. But she'd broken the connection, and there weren't a lot of stations left on the circuit. The voices of Mom, Chuck, the girls, Aunt Loretta, even Jim were growing faint, their calls weak in the static. Soon they would fade out altogether, leaving me in a howling silence where I'd have to deal with the dogwolf at last.

I was up on the roof of the house, nailing down some loose shingles, when I saw him coming down the town road. He was a small man, old but still spry from the way he moved. He didn't seem in any hurry, stopping once to sit on his bag to light a pipe, and pausing again a few dozen paces on to study something by the side of the road. I went back to hammering on the roof, forgetting all about him until suddenly I had the feeling of being watched. I looked up quickly. He was sitting in the shadow of the pump house, smoking his pipe and looking very relaxed. He lifted a hand and waved.

I climbed down the ladder and walked over. *"Bonjour,"* he said. "Hot up on that roof, 'ey?"

"Yeah, it is," I said. "Can I help you?"

"This is the Hendrickson farm, 'ey?"

"Yes," I said uncertainly.

"Might Janice LaSavage live here?"

"Uh, yes. She's Janice Hendrickson now. She's not here right now."

"And you are Pierre?"

"Well, I'm Pete, if that's what you mean."

He got up, dusting off the seat of his faded pants. He smiled, the dark skin around his brown eyes creasing into a thousand wrinkles. "I thought so." He extended a hand. "I'm your grandfather Jean LaSavage. I am glad to see you." I was too dumbfounded to react. "A surprise, 'ey?" He chuckled.

I shook his hand and managed to nod my head. He relit his pipe, his eyes laughing behind the cloud of smoke. "Uh, would you like something to drink?" I asked.

"I had a cup of your water while you were working. It's good water." He looked over the farm. "And this is a good place. Was it my boy's?"

"No, Mom and I moved here after she met Chuck. That was four years after — " I stopped. My God, what did he know? Did he think Dad had just moved on, or did he know the truth?

He smiled sadly, reaching out to touch my arm with a gnarled hand. "I know," he said. "A long time ago, 'ey?"

"Yes," I said.

He looked out over the field rolling toward the ridge and the woods beyond. "This is good country," he said. "It would have suited him." He smiled again. "Go on with your work, Pierre. Young men must work while old men rest, 'ey? I'll sit here and close my eyes for a while."

"You could go in the house. Do you want something to eat?"

"No, here is good, and I ate in town when I stopped for directions." He settled himself again and smiled up at me. "Go on. We will talk later when your mother gets home." He closed his eyes.

I hesitated a moment, thinking that I should offer more but too unsure to know what. I got a drink and then climbed back on the roof. I worked slowly, my mind a jumble. Every once in a while, I'd look over to see if he was still there, almost expecting to find him gone, another apparition in a summer when little seemed real anymore.

I was nearly finished when I saw Mom's car coming down the road. I hammered the last shingle in place, pushed the scraps over the edge, stuck my tools in my work belt, and made for the ladder. Mom had the car parked and was getting the girls out of their seat belts. "You look hot," she said. "I hope you're drinking lots of water."

"Uh, Mom. We've got a guest." I pointed to

where the old man sat in the shade. He was smiling and lighting his pipe.

She frowned. "Who is it?"

"He says he's Grandpa LaSavage."

She stared. "Oh, my God. I thought he was dead."

We sat at the kitchen table while Mom made supper. The girls hung on me, staring at him with big eyes. Mom made nervous conversation: "Where's home?" she asked.

"A little place called Arek, north of Fifty-Four, beyond The Pas on the way to Flin Flon."

Heidi tugged on my arm and whispered, "Why's he talk funny?"

"He's not from around here," I whispered back.

"Is that somewhere around Winnipeg?" Mom asked.

He smiled. "No, a way west and a long way north. As far again as Winnipeg is from here. Close to a thousand miles by road."

"My Lord," Mom said. "Did you ride a bus all that way?"

"No, I hitchhiked. I wait at the truck stops and a driver always give me ride. I'm too old for them to worry about hijacking."

"What's Fifty-Four?" I asked. "A town?"

This time he grinned. "No, no. Not a town. It's the parallel. Above Fifty-Four is God's country."

Heidi tugged on my arm again and whispered, "I thought Daddy said this is God's country."

"He does sometimes," I whispered. Or used to before the fire, I thought.

We heard the Bronco pull into the yard. "Daddy's home," Christine yelped, and ran for the back door. "Beat you," she yelled over her shoulder at Heidi.

"Did not," Heidi shouted, letting go of my arm and charging for the door.

I excused myself and went to tell Chuck that someone none of us had thought about in a long time actually existed.

The old man ate well, complimenting Mom in both English and French on her cooking. After supper we sat outside, the girls on the steps beside me and the rest of them in lawn chairs. He asked polite questions about my school, the girls, Chuck's work, the drought, and the fires in the forest. "I started smelling the smoke full fifty miles north. I knew then that you folks had bad trouble."

"Bad enough," Chuck said. "We've been fighting the fires since spring."

The old man shook his head. "A peat fire. The worst kind. I fought one out in Alberta when I was young. Way north on the Peace River. Ah, it was bad. We lost three good Métis men that summer to the fire."

It was time for the girls to take baths, and the old man said he needed to stretch his legs. When he was out of earshot, I asked Chuck, "What was that word he used? *May-tee* or something?"

"I don't know," he said. "It's French, and I think I heard it a time or two out West, but I don't remember what it means."

It wasn't until an hour later, when the girls were in bed and we were seated again at the kitchen table, that the big questions finally got asked. Mom took a deep breath and said, "Did you ever get my letter about Pete's father?"

The old man studied his folded hands. "Yes, but not for a long time. Not until I stopped in Batoche after I heard that my aunt had died. The priest had her things, and I went through them looking for something I could keep to remember her. And I found your letter and read . . ." He put his hand to his eyes for a moment, then cleared his throat and went on. "I'm sorry that I never wrote. But it was very difficult." He leaned back and smiled sadly at us. "You must understand: Henri's mother and I parted very long ago, and I'd lost track of her and my boy, too. I was many years older than she and very jealous of the years I had left to wander as I liked. Only later did I learn that life is long and that I might have taken a few years to be a good father."

There was a long silence in the kitchen, the night breeze toying with the curtains and the electric clock on the wall slowly unraveling time. At last Mom said, "He spoke of you a few times. I don't think he blamed you for anything. He wasn't like that. He was a happy man until his accident. After that . . ." She let the sentence trail off.

Chuck cleared his throat. "A couple of the men saw him work in the big timber out West. They say he was a hell of a topper. He just got a bad break."

The old man smiled. "Yes," he said. "The work would have suited him. He learned to climb before he could walk, and he loved high places. I remember that." He looked at me. "I see him in you, and I thank God for that. And Janice found a good man. My son would be happy." He put a hand on the table and pushed himself up with a grunt. "Old bones get stiff when they sit too long, and we've had enough talk for one night. Come walk with me, Pierre, while I smoke my pipe."

"I've made up the spare bedroom for you . . ." Mom hesitated and then said uncertainly, "Grandpa."

He grinned. "Call me Jean. That's all I've ever been."

A steady rain fell that night and through the next day. When I got home from the tower, the old man was shucking peas and telling the girls stories while Mom made supper. He winked at me and went on with a story about Little-Man-With-Hair-All-Over and how he'd climbed down a hole to rescue three beautiful Indian girls, killing first a one-headed, then a two-headed, and finally a three-headed monster. It was a good story, and he spun it out until nearly supper time.

"Tell us another one," Heidi begged.

"Yeah," Christine said. "A long one."

He smiled. "When it's your bedtime, I'll tell you how Coyote disguised himself as a clear spring to trick an evil medicine woman."

"Just keep it clean," Mom said. "I've heard a lot of those Coyote stories."

"I never heard of Little-Man-With-Hair-All-Over," I said.

"Oh, there are lots of Métis stories about him," he said.

Chuck came in from the living room and took his place at the table. "Forgive me, Jean, but I've forgotten what a Métis is. I know I've heard the word."

"The Métis?" The old man laughed. "Why, they're the freest race God or the Devil ever put on Earth. Sons and daughters of Cree women and French voyageurs and trappers. And some Scotch traders, too, although we French Métis aren't sure they really count. The Métis weren't half-breeds, but a people unto themselves. Buffalo hunters, traders, and fighters. Have you never heard of Louis Riel and the Northwest Rebellion?"

Chuck shifted uncomfortably, not wanting to offend. "Uh, I think maybe I heard the name once or twice."

Jean scooped mashed potatoes onto his plate. "Ah, now there's a story. Let's see, how do I start telling you about the great Louis Riel." He stared at a spot above our heads. The girls bounced in their seats. "Come on, Jean, tell us," Heidi begged.

Christine grabbed Chuck's arm and whispered loudly, "He tells really neat stories, Daddy."

"Well, let me begin this way," Jean said. "The Métis hunted buffalo to feed the big fur companies: the French Northwest Company out of Montreal and later the English Hudson's Bay Company. We could call everything from the Red River in eastern Dakota to the Churchill River country in northern Saskatchewan our home. It was a good life, and as long as we were important to the white men, they did not try to cheat us too badly. But the fur trade began to play out and the buffalo herds grew thin, and suddenly the whites began to think that they could live better without us. And that made the people angry because we'd kept the whites alive through long winters and helped keep the peace between whites and Indians with wise words to both.

"Louis Riel, who'd gone to the schools of the white man, stood up among the Métis and told them to declare their own country in the Northwest. Let the Canadians or the Americans or all the demons of Hell come, and the Métis would hold it against them all. The Métis named their nation Rupert's Land, raised a flag — a fleur-de-lis and a shamrock on a white background — and learned to sing "The Falcon's Song," a national anthem as proud as any on earth. But the whites would not let the Métis live in peace. In 1884, the white soldiers came to Batoche, on the Saskatchewan River, with their cannons and their Gatling guns to destroy the Métis nation. Many Métis and white soldiers died in the fight, but finally there were too many soldiers and, weeping, the Métis laid down their arms. Louis Riel escaped, but he returned so that the white men would aim their anger at him, not at the people. The white men took him to Regina for trial in a white court where no one knew or would listen to the real truth."

He'd been talking slowly, pausing to eat between sentences, and that's why he surprised me when he turned to stare at me, his words suddenly harsh. *"Les bâtards* hanged Louis Riel in the fall of 1885, but the Métis can hold their heads high today because we fought the white man even when we could not win." His fierce gaze fixed me to my chair, and for a moment it seemed like there were only the two of us in the room. Then he spoke softly, "I am Métis, my son was Métis, and I think you, too, are Métis, Pierre."

"Can I be Métis, too?" Heidi squealed.

"Me, too," Christine said.

He held my eyes with his, and then he turned to smile at them. "You can be honorary Métis. After supper, I'll teach you a Métis song."

They bounced up and down and squealed. "Settle down and eat your supper, girls," Mom said.

Later, when I was clearing the table and Jean had gone outside to smoke his pipe, I asked Mom: "Did Dad ever talk about this Métis thing?"

"No. I don't recall anything like that." She paused. "But you've got to understand how young

167

we were and how much in love. You don't talk much about things like that when you're in love." She looked at me, her eyes glistening with tears. "I love Chuck," she said, "but it's never the same when you're older and sadder."

It rained hard again that night and all the next day, the clouds breaking in late afternoon to let a wet sun shine through the cool after the rain. I hadn't seen Chuck or Mom or the girls so happy and so relaxed in months. We grilled hamburgers outside, and then sat laughing at Jean's stories until dusk. When Mom took the girls in and Chuck went to "sit on my butt in front of the TV for a change," Jean said, "Walk with me, Pierre."

We strolled out across the field toward the ridge. He paused at the burned patch where Jim and I had nearly set half the damned world on fire. I told him what had happened. He grinned. "That fire had you boys dancing a jig, 'ey?" Before I could answer, he broke into a jig, lifting his knees high, spinning, and yipping like he was dancing on fire.

It was so unexpected that for a minute I stood with my mouth open, and then I was laughing harder than I could remember laughing in a long time. Laughing hard for the first time in so long that the sound of it seemed stranger even than the sight of him suddenly young, as if fifty years had dropped away from him and he was no longer an old man but someone I'd lost before I'd really known him, lost when the great crown of a Douglas fir had broken his body far up a tree in the big timber out West. And I turned away then, afraid that I would cry again or start howling like a wolf, howling like my aunt Loretta had once told me I'd howled after my father had dragged himself off to die in the forest where the fires had burned all this summer, their flames slithering through the dry grass, searching out the hidden thicket where his bones lay huddled in the loneliness.

Behind me, my grandfather asked quietly, "How goes it, Pierre?" I shook my head and started walking on toward the ridge.

We sat together on the crest. He didn't ask me anything, only smoked his pipe thoughtfully as we watched the sunset. The rain had dampened the fires, and the smoke lay like gray mist over the forest. Finally, I said, "I'm sorry, Grandfather. Not a lot has made sense lately. I've kind of gotten out of the habit of laughing."

He nodded. "Every young man has a summer like that."

"That's what my great-aunt Loretta says."

He smiled. "Well, then, she must be a wise woman. You must take me to meet her."

I stared at my hands. "Can you tell me about your summer when nothing made sense?"

He chuckled. "It's too long ago to remember. Perhaps you should tell me about yours."

"I wouldn't know where to begin," I said, and surprised myself by beginning anyway.

He listened, and when I'd finished — or finished

all that I could find the words to tell — he waited a long time before asking: "And this dogwolf. You set him loose, 'ey?"

"Yes," I said.

He grunted. "Well, I think you'll have to go after him one of these days." He struck a match and relit his pipe.

"Yes," I said. "I guess maybe I will."

We sat in silence until the sun disappeared behind the smoke and mist lying on the forest. Then he put a hand on my shoulder to help himself to his feet, and we started walking back toward the farm, our boots leaving wet tracks in the grass.

The heat broke and we had showers off and on for a week. The Forest Service called down half the tower jockeys, leaving One-One and several of the other towers empty. I started roofing the toolshed. Chuck was busy catching up on his neglected office work, so I got Jim to lend me a hand. Sometimes the old man climbed up on the roof and worked with us for an hour or so. Then he'd get out his pipe, perch on the peak of the roof, and joke with us or "tell lies" about the life he'd had "north of Fifty-Four." I prodded him for stories about the Métis. I couldn't quite buy that I was a member of a people I'd never heard of before, but I wanted to know more, since trying to be Indian and white at the same time hadn't worked worth a crap.

He always spoke as if he'd been there himself a

century and more before: "Every spring we'd leave our farms to spend the summers on the prairies in our Red River carts."

"What's a Red River cart?" I asked. "A covered wagon?"

"No, no. A two-wheeled cart. Light and strong and much better than those foolish covered wagons you see in the movies. We were the first people to use any kind of cart or wagon on the northern plains. Dozens of families traveled in caravans of three hundred carts and more, trading with the Indians and hunting the buffalo. The Indians called us the 'wagon people' and gave us a sign." He circled the tips of his forefingers together like turning wheels, then drew the right finger down his chest. He laughed. "Half human, half wagon, they called us. Do you boys know any of the sign talk?" We shook our heads, and he looked sad. "Any Chippewa?"

"A few words," I said uncomfortably. Jim nodded.

He sighed. "It's that way all over. None of the young people are learning the old ways." He gazed across the field toward the road and the highway beyond. Then he grinned and said, "Did I ever tell you about the summer I worked for a freighting outfit on Great Slave Lake? . . ."

Jim liked him and liked the stories, but he talked even less than usual. When I asked him what was on his mind, he said: "I'm just waiting."

"For what?"

"The heat, the fire. It's going to come again."

"Maybe not, it often gets cool and rainy around this time of year. The leaves will start changing in two or three weeks."

"It'll come," he said. "You can count on it."

I felt the breeze shift and stood to have a better look at the sky. The clouds had dropped, coming in low and dark over the forest. I turned to Jim, who was wrestling another square of shingles from the scaffold onto the roof. "We'd better cover up. It's going to rain." He nodded and hoisted himself onto the roof. We spread the sheet plastic, and he started stapling it down while I held the end tight so it wouldn't billow.

Grandpa — we'd all started calling him that despite his protests — came out on the back steps. He studied the sky a moment and then sauntered over. "No more work today, boys. Get that stapled down and come in to lunch. Janice left pea soup for us."

Inside, he ladled soup into our bowls. "Radio says showers off and on all afternoon," he said. "Maybe we ought to get out that old pickup of yours and do a little rambling. I haven't seen anything of the country since I got here."

I looked at Jim. "Sure, why not?" he said. "I'm sick of working."

"You were born sick of it," I said.

"Only white man's work." He took a couple of

spoonfuls, then said, "John's home. You wanted me to tell you."

I thought that news over and then said to Grandpa: "Jim's uncle knew Dad better than anybody around here, except Mom. He worked with Dad out West and saw the accident. I thought maybe you'd like to meet him."

He hesitated a moment. "Yes, I suppose that would be right."

Grandpa and I drove over in the pickup, Jim following in his heap. When we pulled up in front of the house, John turned from throwing branches onto a brush pile. He waved, a grin splitting his broad, dark face. I introduced Grandpa and they shook hands. "Glad to meet you," John said. "I knew your son very well. Come into the kitchen. I've got some coffee on."

The four of us sat around the rickety kitchen table. At first, the talk was of the weather, the fires, and John's job trucking pulp south to the big mills in Wisconsin Rapids and Nekoosa and finished paper products as far away as California. That got the discussion onto logging and finally to Dad. John told some of the stories I'd heard before of how Dad had taken to topping like he'd been born to the trade.

John shook his head at the memory. "He was one hell of a topper. Even the guys who'd been at it for years knew that he was the best. And they didn't mind saying so, bragging in the bars in front of the other logging crews of how White Granite had a half-breed kid who could out-climb, out-cut, and out-work anybody in the Northwest. A few times they even made bets on it, and Hank never lost a one. Never came close to losing one. But Hank, he never bragged. He'd only grin and say that he was just a shanty boy still learning the trade. And, you know, I think in a way he was telling the truth. He'd only been at it three summers and who knows how good he could have been if he hadn't had that lousy accident."

There was an awkward pause and then Grandpa said quietly, "I'm glad he loved his work. It's good for a man to do one thing very well."

John nodded. "Not many are that lucky."

"No," Grandpa said. "Not many. Tell me about the accident."

John hesitated, glancing at me. "I'll tell you what I remember, and I think I remember it all, even though I've tried to forget a few times." He dug his Copenhagen tin out of a pocket and spent a minute getting a chew in his mouth. "We were working east of Coeur d'Alene in the Bitterroot Mountains. God, it was beautiful country — high and cool with hardly any bugs to bother us. We'd talk sometimes about bringing our wives out there to live. I was married back then and maybe I'd still be if I'd done it. Hell, I don't remember drinking hardly at all that summer. Oh, a couple of beers after work sometimes, but nothing like what happened after I stopped working there and came back here to try to drink myself to death."

He shrugged. "But that's another story. Anyway, we were cutting Douglas fir, four or five feet on the stump and most of them just as straight as telephone poles. White Granite was a class outfit. A lot of the companies didn't employ more than one or two toppers. Their saw crews would knock down the fir with the crowns still on, and that played hell with the quality of the lumber, because the trunks would flex and split when the crowns hit the ground. But White Granite had a policy of topping most of its trees, and there were half a dozen toppers working out ahead of the saw crews.

"Hank was my crew's topper and usually he worked so fast that we had trouble keeping up. But the day of the accident, he was slower, as if he sensed that the big timber had a trick waiting for him. About an hour after lunch, we came to this big fir, the biggest we'd seen all day. He walked around it slow, which wasn't like him, since it usually only took him a glance to know the best angle to drop a crown. 'What's the matter?' I ask him. He shakes his head: 'I dunno for sure, but I think there's a corkscrew twist somewhere in there. Look how that crown forks. Something ain't right.'

"I look it over and everything looks okay to me, but I say, 'Do you want me to tell the boss that we're gonna drop this one as is?' And he hesitates, not wanting to admit that this one's got him scared.

175

'No,' he says, 'I'll just watch 'er close.' 'Are you sure?' I ask. And he says, 'Yeah, it'll be okay.'

"But it wasn't. There was something inside the bark that we couldn't see. Maybe a soft spot or a lightning score or just some twist that had developed during all the time that tree had been growing big. Hank goes up, quick as a bobcat just like always, clears away a few limbs in his way, and starts cutting the notch. I'm watching close to see if that crown moves before it should, but there's nothing wrong that I can see. He doesn't have to use any wedges to keep his saw from binding, and the notch falls clear without any problem, bouncing in the brush near us. He kicks out and swings around on the safety belt to the backside and begins cutting the hinge. He's maybe three quarters of the way in, chips spitting out of his saw like that tree is made of balsa wood, when I see that crown shudder and start to twist. I try to yell, but it's too late. That crown comes down spinning on the hinge. Hank tries to kick out to get out of the way, but it happens way too fast. The top hits him and swings clear so that I can see it's knocked him maybe six or seven feet down the trunk, and then it swings back and I'm sure it's going to break loose, but instead it just swings back and forth a few more times and then stops with Hank hidden under all the green.

"The boss comes running up, and we start yelling, hoping that Hank's managed to dodge the biggest branches and is clinging to the trunk, banged up but still conscious. But then we spot one of his boots sticking out from under the branches, and he isn't moving at all. Reilly, one of the other toppers, is there by now and he says, 'Who's going up this bastard with me?' And I sure as hell don't want to, because I ain't done much climbing and I hate the height. But I hear myself say, 'I will.' 'Get some spikes and a belt,' he says.

"The boss and the rest of the crew start rigging a sling and I take the rope up when I start climbing. Reilly's up there ahead of me. He peers in through the branches, trying to get a good look at Hank, and then he climbs all the way up and takes a look at the hinge. I'm up level with that hanging crown by then, and Reilly comes back down and says, 'Ain't more than a pencil holding it. I'm gonna have to work slow. If I lose it, we're all gonna be screwed.' I nod, and Reilly starts cutting away the limbs.

"Reilly's maybe the foulest-mouthed man I've ever known. God, none of us were prudes, but Reilly used more swear words than any other kind. All the time he's pruning away those branches, I hear him muttering under his breath, and suddenly I realize that he's not swearing at all. No, he's saying Hail Marys over and over again. I take it up, even though I haven't been to church in years, and then we do an Our Father, and then some more Hail Marys. Finally, he's cut away enough of the branches for me to wriggle in to get at Hank. He's pinned against the trunk by a big limb across

177

his back. Reilly calls, 'Is he alive?' And I say, 'Yeah, he's breathing.' 'Can you hold him while I get this big branch?' he asks. 'Yeah, I can do it,' I say. I hear Reilly take a big breath. 'We're taking a hell of a risk,' he says. 'I know,' I say. 'Okay, then, here we go,' he says and starts cutting. That crown groans and sways and I'm promising God that I'll go to church regular if he can just hold that top up a little while longer. And that branch drops, and Hank falls back against the safety harness and I've got him, and Reilly's almost crying because he's so scared and just choking out the Hail Marys one after another.

"Another topper comes up and somehow we manage to get Hank in the sling. The boss wants Reilly to drive a big eye into the tree and rig a pulley so they can lower Hank from the ground. But Reilly tells him it's too dangerous to start hammering on the trunk because most of that crown is still hanging around us with only that sliver not much bigger than a pencil holding it. So we have to lower Hank a foot at a time, Reilly and me holding on to the rope with one hand each and the other topper going down slow, trying to steady Hank in the sling."

John paused, his voice thick with emotion. "So we got him down, and Reilly and me got out from under that crown alive. Later, Reilly told me that he was never gonna swear again, that he'd promised the Virgin while he was up there figuring that he was gonna die any second. And he never did, or never in my hearing the few times I saw him after that."

He got up to get the coffee pot from the stove. "We took Hank to the hospital in Coeur d'Alene. He was all mashed up: back, pelvis, legs, and bleeding a lot inside. The doctor said that it was a wonder we hadn't killed him just lowering him in the sling, but that Hank was a tough little bugger and that he'd do what he could to pull him through. I called Janice and told her what had happened. That was maybe the hardest part of all."

Suddenly I couldn't take any more. "Uh, I've kind of heard this part. I think I'll sit outside for a while."

I was sitting on the tailgate of the pickup when Jim joined me. "How you doing?" he asked.

"Okay," I said.

"You know all that stuff?"

"Only the outline, not the details."

He shook his head. "Damn. I never knew John climbed that tree. He doesn't even like going up a stepladder. That must have been one special friendship."

"Yeah," I said. "Real special."

"Suppose your Mom knows?"

"I don't think so."

Jim shook his head again. "Damn. That took some real balls."

The two of them came out of the house a while later. They were laughing, but got serious when they came up to us. "Pete," John said, "I'm going

179

to take your grandpa over to the forest to show him where we found your dad's pickup. Do you want to come, or should we drop you by your place?"

"I'll come; it doesn't bother me. But it's been hot in there. We'll have to ask permission at the Forest Service office."

"Should have cooled off by now," he said. "We've had quite a bit of rain."

We rode in John's pickup, driving the round-about way from the rez across the strip of open country to the southern edge of the forest and then north to the Forest Service headquarters. Chuck was in, digging his way through a heap of papers on his desk. "Hey, John. Long time." He stood and they shook hands.

"If it's okay, I'm gonna take Jean and the boys up to the spot where we found Hank's pickup."

"Okay, I guess. But be careful, we've had a hell of a time in there. The fire's been creeping out through the roots of the balsam along the edge of the peat, and we had a pretty big surface burn there about ten days ago. You should be okay, but watch your step. Park off the road so we can get the trucks through if something happens."

"Sure thing. We'll leave you to it then."

Chuck glanced at his littered desk and grimaced. "Yeah. I'd go with you, but I'd better shovel some of this garbage."

We parked off the road behind a backhoe and a big D-9 Cat belonging to Chuck's fire crew. The crews were on stand-down, and only a couple of bored-looking guys were there, sitting under a tree playing gin on a square of oilcloth. "Take it easy if you leave the road," one of them called. "We've still got fire in the roots." John waved.

He led us up the fire lane a quarter mile and then off on the overgrown trace of a logging road for a few hundred yards more. "We found his pickup right about here. In his condition, I don't see how he could've made it far, but we searched for a couple of miles in every direction. And when we didn't find him, we did it again." He shook his head. "But he didn't want to be found, and I guess he knew a good hiding place."

The old man nodded. "That would have been his way." We stood for an awkward couple of minutes.

"Well," John said, "let's walk in for a look at the burn-over and then swing back to the truck."

They walked ahead, talking quietly, while Jim and I hung back, both lost in our own thoughts. The land sloped down toward the peat bog, the heavy timber giving way to a stand of balsam fir along its edge. The bulldozers had hacked a fire-break through the balsams, and we crossed the ruts into the area where the fire had exploded out of the roots to ignite the surface burn. Along the edge of the firebreak, the fire had stripped away the branches, leaving the trunks blackened spears, but closer to the peat we had to climb over charred trunks tumbled like jackstraws. Jim said, "The fire must have eaten the roots clear through. There must have been a hell of a blaze when they started falling."

I was about to reply when I smelled fire under the wet charcoal smell of the burn-over. I spun. Jim caught the smell, too. "Where?" he said.

I dropped to my knees and felt the ground. "Shit, it's hot!" I scrabbled forward on all fours, feeling the ground, then laid my cheek on the ash trying to hear the sizzle of burning roots.

"Back up, Pete! We've got to backtrack."

I jumped to my feet, took a couple of steps, and yelled, "Grandpa! John! Watch out — "

With a whoosh, the fire exploded out of the earth a dozen feet in front of me, the ground caving in around it. I felt Jim grab my arm and pull me back. Through the flames I could see John and Grandpa spin. Then they were running at right angles to the fire. "Come on," Jim hollered.

We ran for the edge of the balsam, the fire ripping out of the ground behind us as we scrambled over the fallen trees. I fell, a jagged branch jabbing into my side. Jim turned to help me. "I'm okay," I yelled. "Go!"

We'd run maybe a hundred yards, when Jim panted, "It's okay. It's way behind."

I turned. The fire was already settling, the flare-up spent as the flames hit the wet ash. "Where are Grandpa and John?" I asked.

"Over there laughing at us." I looked. They were standing on a little hillock, both of them half doubled over with laughter. "I guess they didn't think it was much to worry about," Jim said.

"Guess not."

We heard the sound of the backhoe's engine, and the two guys from the fire crew came bumping over the ruts of the firebreak. "Found one for us?" one of them called. We pointed, and they waved. They looked almost happy to have something to do besides playing gin. We joined John and Grandpa. "God, can you boys move." John laughed. "I wish to hell you moved half that fast most of the time, nephew." Jim glowered at him.

Grandpa reached out a finger and ran it down my smudged cheek. "Now you really are one of the *Bois-Brûlés* — the half-burned men. That's what the voyageurs called the Métis."

We rode in the back of John's pickup. In front the two men were talking and laughing together. "I told you it'd be back," Jim said, staring at the trees flashing past as John accelerated along the blacktop. "And it's going to get a whole lot worse before we're done with it."

The next morning it was ninety by noon, the cloud of smoke from the fires in the forest rising high against the hot blue of a rainless sky.

CHAPTER
EIGHT

The summer got a whole lot harder on everyone.
The heat sucked the moisture out of the ground,
and the leaves on the trees started turning brown.
A hot wind blew out of the west, and every evening
the far horizon crackled with heat lightning.

Chuck started spending nights on a cot at the
Forest Service headquarters, and I started sitting
tower again. Grandpa came with me the first day,
but he was restless and less talkative, his gaze wandering off toward the north. "Time I was heading
home," he said.

"I wish you'd stay a while. Mom really appre-
ciates your help with the girls while Chuck's away."

He smiled. "Yes, the little ones have a shine for
their *grand-père*. Well, let's see what the next two
or three days bring, 'ey?"

The radio crackled. "One-One, this is Crescent
Lake."

I reached through the window for the mike.
"Roger, this is One-One."

"Pete, Mac called in. His wife's feeling kind of

punk, and he wants to take her to the doctor to-morrow morning. He said he'll come over this afternoon if you can take tomorrow morning for him, Over."

"No problem," I said.

"Good, I'll give him a call. Crescent Lake, Out."

I set the mike on the desk and turned back to Grandpa. The old man fidgeted, combing back his white hair with his fingers and squinting through the hot wind at the smoke rising from the forest. "Is that something new?" He pointed to a billow of black smoke far to the west beyond Chuck's sector.

I lifted my glasses and studied the smoke. "No, that one's been burning since yesterday. It looks like they're starting to get a handle on it."

We were silent for a couple of minutes. "Well," he said, "I guess I'll climb down and go back to the farm. See if Janice needs any help."

"Watch out for the wild critters."

He took me seriously. "You mean that wolfdog, 'ey?"

"No, I didn't mean anything. Just kidding."

"I'd rather run into a grizzly than a big dog gone wild. At least you know what to expect from a bear."

"Well, there aren't any grizzlies around here, and I think the dogwolf's long gone. I haven't heard or seen anything of him in a week or two. Probably got run over or shot by now."

"Perhaps, but I heard a dog howl the other night." He pointed in the direction of Wilson's cabin. "From around there, I'd guess."

I felt a twinge in my stomach. "There are lots of dogs around," I said.

He nodded. "True, but maybe we ought to go have a look around this afternoon, 'ey?"

I hesitated. "Okay, I guess. We could try for some red squirrels, anyway." He started for the ladder. "Here," I said, "I'll get the trapdoor for you."

Mac came just before noon, and I climbed down to meet him. He looked glum. "Thanks for changing schedules, Pete. I appreciate it."

"Anytime. How's Phyllis?"

"Not so good. The heat and the smoke are getting to her. She's got it in her head that the big one's going to burn us out one of these days."

"I don't think it'd get as far as your place," I said. "You're quite a way out."

"I know, but she's a worrier, and she's got this respiratory thing. If things get any worse, I may have to get her out of here for a while." He put a foot on the bottom rung of the ladder and stared up at the shack. "Well, we'll see what the doctor says. Thanks again." With a grunt, he started the climb.

Mom had run into town, leaving the girls with Grandpa. I ate lunch and then called Jim to see if he was back from driving John down to Illinois to pick up a new rig for the company. He was. "When'd you get back?" I asked.

"Last night 'round ten. Didn't even have the energy to go over to Eddy's. God, that's a long drive."

"Well, you've got John's pickup for a few days, anyway."

"Right. And he probably copied down the mileage so he'll know if I'm driving it instead of my car."

"Well, if the heap's still running, come on over. Grandpa and I are going hunting."

"Sounds good. Could use a little venison."

"Uh-uh," I said. "Just bring your .22. I don't want to be around when Big Bill catches you with a shotgun."

"Squirrels ain't no challenge," he groused.

"Well, you can take a shot at the dogwolf if we see him."

There was silence at his end. "Somebody should," he said.

I took Grandpa out to the garage to give him a choice of the guns. He smiled when he saw Chuck's old Winchester pump .22. "Now there's a gun, 'ey? Never a better one."

"If you like hammer safeties," I said.

"I do." He reached up to take the rifle out of the rack.

Mom got home about two, and Jim came rattling in ten minutes later. Mom gave us the usual cautions about not shooting each other, and I led the way across the field and over the ridge into the lower forty where we picked up the path to Wilson's. The place looked like it hadn't been inhabited in a dozen years. Bert Weathers or one of the other deputies had come by in the days after we'd found Wilson and tacked up a sign on the door to warn off trespassers. I stepped close to read the fine print, while Jim hung back, glancing nervously around. Grandpa walked over to the cage, pausing to study the ground. "Something plenty big's been here," he said. I went over to look. A line of tracks led to the cage door, hesitated, took a step inside, turned, and then disappeared across the hard-packed earth toward the woods. Grandpa knelt and measured one of the tracks with his palm. He whistled. "That is some big dog, 'ey?"

"And big-time dumb, too," I said, although I no longer believed it.

"He's getting by," Grandpa said. "A lot of dogs can't make it in the wild." He studied the cage. "The old guy had money, 'ey?"

"Not that I know of. Probably just Social Security."

He shook his head. "Just that floor took a lot of cash. That's four inches of solid concrete. He didn't want that wolfdog digging its way out." He started following the tracks toward the woods.

"Wilson didn't pay for it," Jim said quietly.

I looked at him. "How do you know?"

"There's talk up at Eddy's. Seems Wilson told a couple of the old guys that he got it from some crazy priest. Wilson got a check for fifty bucks every month he kept the dog."

"A real priest?" I asked.

"That's what Wilson said. Said he tried to give the damned thing back after he found out how mean it was, but the priest'd run off."

"I don't believe it," I said. "Wilson was always full of crap. I'll bet he got it from a pound somewhere. Was that what you were trying to find in the cabin? Something about the priest?"

"Something like that."

Grandpa came back from following the tracks. "I think he's lying up somewhere close. Close enough to keep an eye on the place." He looked at me. "You're going to have trouble with that beast before long, Pierre. Perhaps we should look for it, 'ey?" I hesitated and then nodded.

Without snow or blood, there was no easy way to track the dogwolf from the point where his tracks disappeared into the trees. We poked into deadfalls and thickets for two hours, trying to find where he was lying up. Jim hung back, nervously fingering his rifle. Finally, we came to the edge of the swamp where the three tall pines overhung the granite island. I didn't think the old man would risk the tricky footing, but after squatting for a few minutes to smoke his pipe, he stood and started casting about for a path across the muskeg.

"I know a way, Grandpa. I've been out there."

I led them across, the moss spongy under our feet and the mosquitoes swarming around us. The pines threw shadows across the boulders, and even in the buzzing heat there was something still and cold about the place. Grandpa studied the climb into the rocks and then shook his head sadly. "I'm too old for it, boys. You'll have to go up without me."

I glanced at Jim. He shook his head and looked away. "You won't find him now. Only in the dark."

I went up alone, my stomach knotting with fear. I'd started this climb before but had found an excuse to turn back. But this time I had to do it, had to know for certain if this was the place where all the shadows of my nightmares resolved into one. I edged around to the right to get downwind, losing sight of Jim and Grandpa. A gust of hot breeze brought the smell of blood, shit, and rotting flesh eddying down from the rocks. I crouched, tasting vomit in my throat and feeling the sweat prickling between my shoulder blades. I slid the bolt of my rifle back to make sure that I'd chambered a bullet, took a deep breath, and moved.

I heard a whine of terror and knew it was my own as I lurched out of the shadow of the boulders, swinging the rifle barrel wildly from side to side and trying to look everywhere at once. Nothing. No blood-lust snarl, no sudden rushing shape, no flashing teeth and hot stinking breath before the bone-cracking impact as he hit me. Just silence beneath the sighing of the wind in the pine branches and the hammering of my own heart. I slumped back against a boulder, my legs shaking so hard that I could barely stand.

After a minute, my brain cleared, and I could take in my surroundings. Some force too huge and too long ago to imagine had hollowed the top of the outcropping into a bowl a dozen yards across, its floor a tilting slab of granite cracked and gouged by ten thousand winters and springs of hard freeze and slow thaw. Grass grew in scattered patches, clinging to the wind-blown soil in the hollows and crevices. Lichens splotched the shadowed sides of the tumbled boulders ringing the bowl, and I nearly missed the outline of figures beneath. My breath caught, and for a second I forgot about the dogwolf and my fear and all the other things that had turned me into a quivering jellyfish in the months since spring. I stepped closer to one of the boulders, reaching out to peel away the lichens.

The figures were faint, almost unrecognizable as animals and men after the centuries of rain and wind wearing away the rock. But they were there all right, etched into the hard stone with unbelievable patience. At the bottom of the drawing, a warrior with long unbound hair lay crushed, while a huge bear turned to face the other hunters. I reached out and laid a finger gently on the warrior's body, wondering if he had been laid to rest here in this place, beneath a sun and a sky that had never seen white men or Métis or half-breed kids like me.

The hot wind eddied again, and the smell of rotting flesh jarred me back to reality. I turned quickly, bringing the gun back up. The dogwolf wouldn't lie out in the open. No, he'd find shelter in the shaded rocks around the hollow. He could be watching me now, head up, unblinking eyes gauging the distance between us. I looked for the source of the rotting-meat smell. Had he dragged something here? Or maybe it was the dogwolf himself. Perhaps he'd been shot and had struggled back to the rocks to die. I moved slowly, searching the shadows between the boulders, my ears straining for the slightest sound — the click of a claw, the rattle of a pebble, anything that would give me a split-second warning before the dogwolf burst from his hiding place, muscles gathering for the spring at my throat.

I found the torn body of a fawn lying in a hollow between two large boulders on the far side of the bowl. The smell was very bad, and I thought of tying my bandanna around my nose, but I was unwilling to set down my rifle even for a moment. I moved to the right, peering cautiously into every possible hiding place in the jumble of boulders. Finally, I stood by the pictograph of the broken hunter again, knowing for certain that the dogwolf wasn't here but that he had been and would be again when next his killing was done. I unzipped my fly and urinated on the granite to let him know that I'd heard him calling and that I'd come to find him.

When I scrambled down from the rocks, Grandpa asked, "Did you find anything?"

"No, not for certain," I said. Jim looked at me oddly, his eyes half questioning, half knowing.

That night at supper, Grandpa said that he had to be getting back north. The girls put up a fuss, and Mom said that he couldn't go until he'd met Aunt Loretta.

We drove over to the rez the next afternoon after Mac relieved me in the tower. Aunt Loretta seemed older and frailer than ever, and Grandpa looked almost youthful beside her. Before Mom could introduce him, the old woman smiled and said, "It's that devil boy's father. I'd know him anywhere." She brushed aside his proffered hand, stepped close and reached up to put her withered hands on either side of his face. She gazed into his eyes. "Yes," she said. "The eyes are the same. It is well that neither one of us is young anymore. I'm not sure I could resist."

"We are not that old." He laughed.

"Ah, a devil like your son. Come in and sit close to me so that I can hear you."

I sat sipping my glass of iced tea while they talked and the girls dug through the yarn basket. When I'd finished, I rose. Mom gave me a stern look, but Aunt Loretta waved. "Let him go, Janice. Let him go."

I walked downtown to see who was around. As usual, Harney had the street pretty much to himself. "I'll buy this time," I called, and went into the trading post for sodas.

When I gave him his, he grumped, "About time you paid for a little of that advice, scout."

"Call it even now?"

"Not hardly." He took a swallow and belched. "Been up to see your great-aunt?"

"Yeah. She sticks kind of close to home now, but she's feeling okay, I think."

"That's good. Haven't seen her since the dance, and I'd started to wonder."

"What'd you think of it?"

"Oh, it was a hell of a good powwow. I did a lot of business. Say, did you hear Hannah Twodeer ran off with that Kiowa shaman? Left a note for her kids saying that she'd be back in a couple of days, and no one's seen her since." He laughed. "Quite a hustler that shaman."

I took the opening. "I was talking to Aunt Loretta a while back, and she said your uncle was the last *midé* shaman around here."

"She did, huh?" He wasn't laughing anymore.

"Was he?"

"Nah, he wasn't no shaman. He was a drunk, half-crazy old fool who couldn't cast a spell to save his ass. The people laughed at him, and nobody was afraid of him except little kids whose parents said that he'd come and get them if they didn't behave."

"But Aunt Loretta said that Father Shannon — "

"Father Shannon was a cranky old priest who

couldn't stand anybody disobeying him. He dragged my uncle into the street because he wasn't going to mass and because he was mumbling crazy stuff that no one believed except Shannon himself. Hell, people laughed at them both. They were a pair."

"Aunt Loretta seems to think that Father Shannon was pretty special."

"Well, he was better than some, I guess. A lot of the people liked him, but I could never forgive him for what he did to that young minister who built the little chapel up in the woods north of town."

"What'd he do to him?"

"Well, hell, that young guy wanted to build his chapel here in town. And even though he was full of crap, he was harmless enough. No threat to Shannon or anybody, but Shannon made a big fuss with the committee and talked them into keeping the minister from building here. So the committee told that kid that he could build his chapel way up there in the boonies, not expecting him to be fool enough to do it. But he was. And then when people started worrying about him that winter, Shannon tells 'em to stay away. So, when Jamie Lonetree finally did check on him, that youngster's too far gone with cold, hunger, and loneliness to save. Shannon goes up there, then, and sits with him until he's sure he's dead, while the guys who went along have to sit out in the cold because Shannon says that what he and that kid have to say is private. I think that youngster's death was on the old fart's conscience the rest of his life. It damned well should have been."

I stared at Harney, no longer knowing what the truth really was. "Okay," I said. "How about the young priest who followed Father Shannon? Aunt Loretta said there was a rumor that he read something in Father Shannon's diary that drove him crazy. She said that she didn't believe it, but that a few people did."

"I know what you're driving at, scout, and you're way off. Father Shannon didn't know anything about the old sorcery and he didn't care. He didn't leave any diary that drove that young priest *windigo*. That young priest was a queer. He was trying to diddle some of the boys, and Strawback's dad — who was twice the man his kid'll ever be — told the bishop to get his ass out of here before somebody stuck a knife in him."

"How do you know?"

"Because I was there, scout, and the bishop took one look at me and figured out who had the knife. So they got that young priest out of town and put out the story that he needed help for a drinking problem, which he probably did, but that wasn't the reason they took him away. Hell, he used to show up here at the powwows for years afterward to moon over the boys and the young men dancing. But a lot of people knew the truth by then, and nobody'd have anything to do with him."

I took a deep breath. "Well, let me ask one more.

Do you believe there was anything to the *midéwiwin* sorcery? Did any of the spells really work?"

Harney studied me. "Let me put it this way, scout. Enough people believed in them that it didn't make a lot of difference. They thought they worked, so when a shaman let out that he'd sent a spell to give somebody a twisted mouth or paralyzed legs or the falling-down sickness, that's what happened to them. That's why we're a hell of a lot better off now that most of that old stuff is forgotten. Young Strawback and the others are damned fools for even talking about bringing it back. We've got a pretty good thing going here what with the government aid and the foolish tourists throwing their money around. Strawback and his boys think they can screw more out of the government by invoking a lot of traditional rights. It's all goddamn politics to them. Hell, they even came to ask me what I knew of the *midéwiwin*. I told them to buzz off. Just like I told your young lady when she showed up asking if my uncle had taught me how to make a love charm."

I was dumbfounded. "Mona asked you for a love charm?"

"That's right, scout. And then she got mad when I wouldn't talk to her and said she'd make one herself. Been feeling any longings?"

"Not of that kind."

Harney snorted. "The hell you ain't. But relax, scout, you're just horny. Ain't got nothing to do with love charms, just hormones. Now it's time for you to toddle along, scout. I gotta rest up in case the tourists start coming." He leaned back and closed his eyes.

I started away and then turned back. "Harney, do you believe in anything?"

His eyes came open, and they were hard. "Not that it's any business of yours, scout, but I believe in the Chief Joe Harney Indian Relief Fund. Do you know how much I've got in there, boy?"

"No."

"Well, you ain't gonna, either, but I'll tell you this. In another three years, the Chief Joe Harney Indian *Retirement* Plan is gonna kick in, and this here Indian is going to spend the winters someplace warm. Now go away, boy. This wise old chief doesn't have any wisdom that he hasn't already given you. I thought you were smarter than the rest, that maybe you'd figured out which way the wind's blowing."

"I haven't a clue."

"Well, too bad for you. Go think about it." He leaned back and closed his eyes again. I was half-way down the porch when he spoke softly: "Scout." I turned. He didn't open his eyes. "Don't mess with what you don't understand. There are things out there that can tear your heart out, and you'll never find it again."

He made a gesture as if to brush away a fly, and for a moment my vision seemed to flicker, the street turning suddenly gray like an old-time photograph. I blinked and the gray was gone as quickly as it had come, leaving the street as bright and still as before. I stared at Harney, saw the black slits of his eyes watching me, and felt the hair on the back of my neck stiffen. Harney shifted his rump to get more comfortable, sighed, and began to snore softly — faking it so I wouldn't ask what he'd done.

After supper, I joined Grandpa beside the pump house where he sat smoking his pipe as he had on that first afternoon he'd come down the road. He stretched and smiled. "Good traveling day tomorrow. If I start at daybreak, I can make Winnipeg by evening and be north of Fifty-Four day after tomorrow."

"I guess," I said.

He reached over and patted my knee. "Have to go, Pierre. If I don't get home before long, Mert'll get over missing me."

"Who's Mert?"

"My gal. She puts me up, gives me work around her motel, and buys me beer. Not too bad, 'ey?"

"I never imagined. . . ."

He smiled at me sadly. "Perhaps I told you too many stories of the old-time Métis. Did you think I still lived like one of them?" I shrugged. "When I was younger, I tried, Pierre. Tried as hard as any man could when most of what we had left was stories of how things used to be. I worked dozens of jobs all over the North, trying to live free when I should have settled down and been a decent husband and father. But a man gets tired, Pierre. After a while, you can't do the hard jobs anymore. These days, Saturdays fishing and one night a week on the town are about all the excitement I can stand. Otherwise, it's TV and early to bed just like most old people. I'm still Métis, Pierre. And Mert's Métis. We remember the old stories and songs, and we tell them and sing them to those who will listen. And in between we have a good, quiet life with our memories." He patted my knee again. "You come visit sometime. We'll catch some fish and tell some lies, 'ey?"

"Sure," I said.

He put a hand on my shoulder and worked himself stiffly to his feet. "Now let's go in and talk a while with the family. The little ones are going to miss their *grand-père*." He paused, staring at the sunset. *"Entre chien et loup."* I looked at him questioningly. "Twilight," he said, "what the Métis call the time between the dog and the wolf." His sharp eyes studied me. "You take care with that big animal, whatever it is, Pierre. I did not like the feel of him."

After the girls had heard again how Little-Man-With-Hair-All-Over had rescued the three Indian girls from the monsters, Grandpa paused and then started again very softly: "There was a man who so loved the wind that he kept it in a shoe box buried deep in his closet. But at night the wind would cry and shake the lid of the box until the noises frightened the man's wife and child. So one night, the man took the box outside and let the wind go. And for a time his wife and child were happy. But the wind came back, shaking the windows, rattling in the chimney, and calling under the eaves. And the man's wife and child were afraid. So the man went outside, and the wind took him, blew him down a hundred roads, and carried him across thousands of miles where men had never built roads. And one day, when the man was old, it brought him back and left him where he'd begun. But the man's wife and child had gone away long before. And the old man was left with nothing except the weight of his years and his memories, and now and then, a whisper of the wind he had so loved." He paused, his old eyes watching me. "*Finis.*"

"I didn't like that one," Heidi complained. "I want to hear about Little-Man-With-Hair-All-Over."

"Yeah, me too," said Christine. "Tell us something funny."

He watched me, and then he turned to them. "Well then, *mes enfants*, did I ever tell you . . ."

I glanced at Mom and Chuck. Mom was staring at her work-roughened hands lying open in her lap, while Chuck gazed out the window into the night.

We waited at the side of the highway in the dawn. The old man sat on his bag, pulling gently at his pipe while I fidgeted, unable to put into words all that I wanted to say, all that I had yet to ask. Cars passed, but Grandpa didn't stick out his thumb. "We'll wait for a truck, 'ey? Catch a ride with some driver who's been up all night and needs some stories to keep him awake." A big rig came over the crest of the hill and down toward us. The old man stood. "Ah, here we are." He put out his thumb, and sure enough, the truck changed gears and started to slow. With a hiss of air brakes, it came to a halt twenty yards beyond us. I grabbed his bag, and we jogged to the passenger door as the driver swung it open.

Grandpa hoisted his bag onto the seat. *"Bonjour, mon ami,"* he called. "Good morning, my friend." He turned to me and put his hands on my shoulders. *"Au revoir,* Pierre. Someday, come north of Fifty-Four, 'ey?" I nodded, tears stinging my eyes. He pulled me to him for a moment, and then clambered up into the truck. He turned, his hand swinging the door closed. "Do not forget, Pierre." The gears ground, smoke poured out of the truck's twin stacks, and he was gone, leaving me alone by the road.

Jim called that evening. "Harney's dead. Thought you'd like to know."

I took a deep breath. "How?"

"Story is that he got drunk and choked on his own vomit. I don't know. Maybe he looked at himself in the mirror for the first time in years, grossed himself out, and died."

For a long moment, I couldn't think of anything to say. "I guess the trading post will need a new Indian," I said faintly.

"Yeah. Well, they probably won't have any trouble finding somebody to take the job. Hey, I'll talk to you."

"Sure," I said.

I sat in the tower again the next day, watching the smoke over the forest as the wind blew steadily from the west and, somewhere far away, a little old man made his way north of Fifty-Four. That night I dreamed of the fire exploding out of the ground to chase Jim and me. Forms convulsed in the flames, faces twisting out of shape too fast for me to recognize. And I came awake sweating and terrified, sure that the howl that had broken through my nightmare had been real this time — real and more terrible than the many-faced fire. He was out there, howling for me. And he would keep howling, keep killing, until I joined him.

CHAPTER
NINE

I walked home late under a gibbous moon glaring orange through the smoke haze. Needles and shadows crackled under my feet along the path through the head-high red pine of the lower forty. A cloud drifted across the moon, and I followed it up the ridge, reaching the top as the moon broke clear. On the far side of the dry field, the yard light threw a circle of white between the dark garage and the house, where the crossed yellow of the kitchen window shone. And I did not want to go there, did not want to cross the field into the light of what I had known, almost forever now, as home.

Behind me, the shadows shifted in the red pine and I felt the darkness reaching out. I wanted to go back there, wanted to leave my clothes and my rifle on the ridge and slip naked into the shadows where there was silence and darkness and the chittering, quick-footed sounds of small night creatures scampering for their lives at the soft pad of a predator.

I heard it then, the rustle of something big moving in the pines. I turned slowly, the weight of my rifle too heavy to lift, and listened for the next rustle, the next ripple of breath. A cloud brushed the moon, fell away to the east in a breeze acrid with smoke, and for a moment I thought a darker shape moved with the cloud shadow sliding along the edge of the red pine. But I could not tell for certain, and then there was only the silence and something else pulled at me, drew me across the field toward the light.

I hadn't seen Chuck to talk to in three days when the Bronco pulled into the yard in the morning. He got out and stared disgustedly at the thick coating of yellow dust on the Bronco. "Hi, Pete," he said. "Hose down the truck and then fill the windshield washer for me, will you?"

"Sure," I said.

"And check the oil while you're at it. Ought to be changed, but I don't have time. Any breakfast left?"

"Should be." He went into the kitchen, and I got the hose from the far side of the house. I'd filled the window washer and was checking the oil when he came out and sat on the steps with a cup of coffee and a plate of ham and eggs. "Rough night?" I asked.

"They're all rough now. Cripes, it's dry. I didn't think it could get any drier, but it has. We're hitting every little flare-up with everything we've got, and we're still just keeping ahead of it. God help us if we don't get rain this week."

"Forecast say anything good?"

He shook his head. I closed the hood, picked up the hose, and turned the nozzle full on. He watched, chewing his food, as I sluiced the dust off the Bronco. "Close the windows?" he asked.

"Sure. What do you take me for?"

"A teenager. Which isn't the same as an idiot, but close enough."

"Only the white ones," I said. "Us Métis boys are pretty sharp."

"Bought into that, huh?"

"Some, not a lot."

He grunted. "Well, I miss the old boy. Seems like he brought us some good luck for a while. Now it's the same old thing." He got up with his empty plate. "Coffee?" he asked.

"Sure," I said.

I wiped down the windows and the headlights. Chuck came across the yard and handed me a mug. "Well, I got the top layer off, anyway," I said.

"Thanks, that helps." He glanced at his watch. "I've got to take a shower and get back. You sitting tower today?"

"No, Mac's on."

"Maybe you'd better go after the brush along this end of the drive, then. It bothers me to have it growing so close to the road. A fire'd sweep right across, and you guys could be hard pressed to get out as it is." He paused, brooding. "Your mom's getting nervous. She's talking about taking you guys over to the rez until this is over."

206

"I couldn't go. Mac can't sit every day with Phyllis feeling bad."

He nodded. "Well, Janice isn't ready to go yet. Try to keep the load off her." He glanced at his watch again. "I've gotta hurry." He looked at me, his face worried. "I'm sorry to lay so much on you, Pete."

"It's okay. I can handle it."

He slapped me on the shoulder. "Yeah, I know you can."

I'd been working all summer, but the long handle of the brush hook blistered my palms anyway. I swung the heavy blade in short arcs, hacking through the stems of the alder and raspberry. A few minutes before, I'd clipped a rock hidden in the weeds and nicked the hook so that now the jagged notch caught on the brush every third or fourth swing. I swore, backed out of the brush, and examined the blade. I'd have to get the bench grinder going and resharpen it.

I leaned the brush hook against an old fence post and took the bandanna off my forehead to wring the sweat out of it. Beyond the garage, I could see the girls picking raspberries in the patch on the edge of the woods along the hay field. The bushes didn't have many berries this summer, but finding them kept the girls out of the way while Mom hung wash on the line by the house. I retied my bandanna, picked up the brush hook, and trudged toward the garage, my headache pounding and my palms stinging with the rising blisters.

Heidi screamed and then Christine screamed and they were running across the grass, their pails overturned behind them and their mouths open as they screamed and screamed again. I ran, sprinting to cover the distance to get between them and the dark bolt I expected to see hurtling out of the woods after them. I got there, felt them running on toward the house and heard Mom calling to them. I waited, the brush hook held high, but he didn't come and I didn't hear anything except the buzzing heat of the woods and my sisters crying in Mom's arms. Come on, you bastard. Here I am. No gun, so the odds are even now. Come on, give it a shot, you goddamn coward. But there was nothing — just the sound of half a dozen yellow jackets buzzing in one of the overturned berry pails.

Mom had them pretty well calmed down by the time I walked over to the steps. My guess was that one, maybe both of them, had been stung by yellow jackets. But Heidi had a different story: "It was black, Momma," she whimpered. "Big and black and it snorted at us. Like a bear."

"What's a bear snort like?" Mom asked.

Heidi made a sound more like a pig than anything. "That wasn't it," Christine said. "It sounded more like . . ." She made a sound almost exactly like a pig.

"Was not," Heidi yelled. "You didn't even hear it."

"I did, too!"

"Well, then you didn't see it. Only I saw it."

Mom looked at Christine. "Did you see it, Chrissy?"

Christine shuffled. "Nooo. But I heard it. I heard it just as good as she did, and it sounded . . ." She made a different grunting sound.

Mom looked at me. I shrugged. "I don't know. It could've been several things. Or maybe it was nothing. Just a shadow."

"Was not," Heidi yelled. "I saw it!" She started crying again, which touched off Christine. Mom hugged them to her, murmuring soft comforting words. After a couple of minutes, she got them calmed down again and took them inside for Kool-Aid. I walked over to the trough by the pump house to dunk my head.

She came out again a few minutes later, her face set. "I can't handle this anymore. I'm taking the girls to Aunt Loretta's in the morning. We'll stay there until it rains." I nodded. "I want you to come, too," she said.

"I can't, Mom. Not now."

She tightened her lips. "You're only fifteen. The Forest Service can find somebody else to sit tower when Mac can't."

"That's not all of it, Mom. I just can't go now. I've got a stake in this." I waved a hand helplessly at the gray cloud hanging over the forest. "Even if I'm too young to be on a fire crew, I've got to be part of this."

She studied me for a long moment, then the rigidness seemed to leave her all at once, and she sighed. "You're certain?"

"Yes."

"All right," she said. "I don't understand and I wish you'd come, but I can't force you. Not anymore." She turned and walked back toward the house, no longer looking erect and proud but somehow beaten down and sad.

She gave me a lecture in the morning over breakfast before I left for the tower. Chuck came home for a few hours to help her pack and then he took them to Aunt Loretta's in the Bronco. That night, I came home to an empty house, ate supper, and then sat on the steps watching the heat lightning on the horizon. The phone rang about nine. It was Mac. "Pete, I've got to get Phyllis out. We're going down to Eau Claire for a while. I'm sorry, but there isn't anything else I can do."

"It's okay," I said. "I'll handle the tower."

There was a pause. "You get out quick if the big one gets going. One-One will be right in the path if the wind's from the west."

"I know," I said. "I will."

For two days, I sat tower without seeing anyone. We had thunderstorms in the night, and each morning a half dozen new fires burned in the forest, their smoke black and then fading to gray in the afternoon as the fire crews beat them down with water hoses and bulldozers. On the morning of the third day, Steve came on the radio: "East stations, this is Crescent Lake. We've got another missing-person bulletin from the sheriff. Indian boy, eight years old, last seen near the North Fork road on the rez about seven last night. Keep an eye open to your east."

I froze. After a long minute, I picked the mike off the desk. "Crescent Lake, this is One-One. Have you got a name, Steve?"

"Roger, One-One. Boy's name is Paulie Halfaday. He was picking berries with his sisters and must have wandered off."

Another station keyed a mike. "One-One, this is One-Three. Pete, would that be one of Ade Halfaday's kids from the lumberyard over on the rez?"

My throat was dry. "Yeah, that'd be the youngest, I think."

There was a muffled curse. "God, Ade's gonna be outta his mind. That's up where they've been having trouble with that wolfdog, isn't it?"

"Affirmative," I said.

Some other stations wanted to get in on the conversation, but Steve broke in. "Knock it off, guys. Go out and have a look. Crescent Lake, Out."

I went around to the back side of the deck and

studied the woods with the binoculars. My stomach was tight, and my knees felt weak. If the dog-wolf got that kid, I'd never be able to live with myself again.

It was midafternoon when Steve came back on the radio. "All stations, this is Crescent Lake. They got him, boys. Bert Weathers found him wandering along County Trunk M about half an hour ago. He's okay. Tired, hungry, and scratched up some, but nothing that won't heal." There were a couple of cheers and an "Allll riiight, Crazy Horse." Steve came back on, laughing. "Okay, guys. Who says this job isn't fun sometimes? Don't answer that. Back to work."

I felt tears on my cheeks.

When I got home, I thought of driving over to the rez after supper. But the strain of watching and waiting had tired me out, and I almost fell asleep over my plate. I did the dishes and went to bed, sleeping through a hot, still night.

All the fires were under control in the morning, and I sat relaxed with my feet up on the rail of the deck. The radio hissed, only the occasional message breaking the silence. I ate lunch and settled back in my chair again, the binoculars on my lap. The afternoon slipped by with only a couple of sightings by other towers of new smoke.

Jim came into the clearing when the sun was well down in the west. He leaned his shotgun against a tree and started the climb. I went to open the trapdoor. "How's it going?" I asked.

"It's happening," he said.

"Coffee?"

"No, not now." We took our usual positions on the deck, me on the chair, Jim cross-legged with his back against the rail. "Heard the new forecast?" he asked.

"Not yet."

"Storm coming in from the southwest. A bad one. Heard it on the car radio."

I scanned the horizon. "Don't see anything now."

"You will. Hear about the Halfaday kid?"

"Yeah. He's okay, huh?"

"Yeah, he's okay. Scared shitless, but okay. Said something followed him all night long."

I snorted. "If you were eight and lost in the woods, you'd probably start imagining things, too."

"Why are you so sure he's imagining things?"

"Aren't you?"

"No. I think something did follow him, and we both know what. Wilson wasn't enough for it; it wants somebody else."

I stared at him. "That's *windigo*, Jim. And you goddamn know it."

He watched me, his black eyes flat, and then turned away to gaze out across the trees toward the smoke cloud over the forest. His voice was tired. "You don't get it. You never did and maybe you never can." He tapped the steel rail. "This is surface stuff, white man's crap. This tower, that highway over there, the farms, all of it. What really matters is below the surface, way down deep where things don't work like they teach you in school. The *Anishinaabe* used to have a way to touch it, but we've forgotten how and now we're just as helpless as the white man. But we'd better find that way again, boy. And we'd better find it damned quick, or the whole goddamn world is gonna burn up one of these days."

I started to say, "Oh, bullshit," but the words caught in my throat.

He turned to look at me again. "You remember when we slept in the car out by the old chapel? Well, after you left, I went and sat all day and all that night by that bear skull in the tree. And about dawn it started to glow, man. Glowed like it was full of fireflies, and there were sparks in its eyes. And if I'd had the guts to stay there, maybe I could have reached below the surface. Maybe Bear would have shown me how. But I was too chicken to take the risk and I jumped up and I ran. I blew it."

"Jim," I said, "you hadn't slept — "

"Damn it! Just listen for once."

I held up my hands. "Okay."

"Just listen," he said softly. "Just try to hear before it's too late for both of us." He looked down at his hands and then took a deep breath. "I gotta go."

When I opened the trapdoor for him, he looked

at me a last time, his eyes cold as stone. "Why'd you do it, Pete?"

"Do what?"

He stared at me for a long moment, then shook his head, and started down the ladder. "Hey, I'll see you later," I called after him. He didn't reply. On the ground, he paused to work the leather thong from his long hair so that it fell over his shoulders like the unbound hair of a warrior going into battle. Then he picked up his shotgun and disappeared into the woods.

Steve came on the radio a few minutes later to read the revised forecast, his words falling into the silence as all the tower jockeys turned their binoculars to the southwest to study the horizon blistering with storm clouds.

Thunder shook the house. I lay awake, watching the lightning etching the pattern of the window curtain on the wall. A truck down-shifted for the climb up the long hill on the highway. Its engine protested, backfiring. I wondered where it was bound. Perhaps to Winnipeg and then west and a long way north, where somewhere beyond Fifty-Four it would pass a motel where an old Métis would raise a gnarled hand to wave and wish the anonymous trucker *bon courage*.

When I couldn't stand the waiting any longer, I got up, dressed, and went downstairs. The power was off, and I packed what I could find in the refrigerator by the light of a flashlight. A clap of thunder rattled the windows, and a gust of rain swept across the shingles and was gone. I wrapped the food in my slicker and opened the back door. Dust swirled in the yard, undampened by the brief scatter of rain.

I crossed the field by the flash of the lightning. At the top of the ridge, I paused to study the western sky over the forest. At least a half dozen new fires glowed against the dark underbellies of the clouds. If two or three got together, we'd have the big one. Rain, damn it, I thought. But the clouds only cast down more fire.

I reached the tower in the first faint light. At the base of the ladder, I took several deep breaths; I was going to be one very vulnerable Métis boy until I was in the shack and seated in the grounded chair by the chart table. I climbed fast, feeling the air around me crawling with electricity and expecting any moment the blinding flash of the last lightning I'd ever see. I pushed through the trap-door and scrambled on my hands and knees to the chair. I sat there panting and sweating, while the lightning flashed beyond the windows. God, I was crazy beyond all belief.

When I'd caught my breath and calmed my fear, I turned on the radio and shifted to the fire-fighting channel. The voices crackled out of the forest tense and angry. Half the sectors needed support, but nobody had any to spare. I heard Chuck arguing with headquarters: "This is Fire Three. Look, I've got to have another fire team with at least two more bulldozers and three more tankers. It's that or I'm going to have to pull my boys back to fire lane three-seven-one and try to make a stand there."

Steve came on soothing but worried. "Chuck, this is Steve. I just got in. Charlie's working on it. Just hold the line as well as you can."

"I'm not going to have any line left in an hour unless I get those Cats and tankers, Steve."

"I know, Chuck. We've got problems all over."

Fire Five broke in. "Steve, tell somebody to call those bastards at regional. If we don't get big time support in here, we're going to lose the whole damned works."

"Roger, Fire Five. We're talking to them. Just hold the line."

An anonymous voice broke in. "Keep telling us that and I'm going to come in and shove that goddamn mike right up your ass."

Steve lost his temper. "Goddamn it, guys. We're doing the best we can here. Just hold on; help's on the way."

After that, the calls were all business for the next hour. The band of thunderstorms cleared off to the east, leaving pillars of black smoke rising against a gray sky. Steve turned the mike back to Charlie. I glanced at my watch and flipped over to the tower frequency. Steve came on the air. "All stations, this is Crescent Lake. Who's up?"

I keyed the mike. "This is One-One, you're loud and clear." The other stations started answering.

In fifteen minutes, everybody was on the air. Steve started the briefing. "Okay, guys. As you can see, we're having a very bad time of it. We've got four majors and God knows how many small fires. Nothing's under control yet, but help's on the way. So just do your jobs and keep the chatter down. The band of storms that gave us all the trouble is clear now, so you should be able to move around. But we've got another band of heavy storms due in late this afternoon, so get ready to ride the hot seats between four and five or five-thirty."

He paused. "Okay, big problem, guys. As it starts getting warmer, we're looking at thirty-mile-per-hour winds out of the west southwest, gusting to forty miles per. That means we're going to have trouble holding the fires down, and you're going to have to watch for windblown sparks. So sweep full circle and keep doing it." He paused again. "Now, I know some of you guys like to flip over to the fire-fighting channel every once in a while to hear the action. But this is one day when everybody obeys all the rules. Stay on this channel, and this channel only. Any questions?"

There were a few questions, but no smart-ass comments. I opened the window and dragged my chair onto the deck. Steve came back on: "One more thing, guys. If the fire breaks into open country, you guys on the east get ready to pull out on the double quick. That fire will be moving faster than you can run, and you'll need all the head start you can get."

The message traffic was heavy all morning, the towers on the north and west transmitting a stream of new sightings. As predicted, the wind picked up with the heat, and it was blowing hard by mid-morning. For the first time, I began picking out the ripple of flames as hot gases exploded in the swirling smoke columns. The columns listed to the east with the wind, eddied, and then slowly, because there wasn't anything that could stop them now, merged into a huge tilting cloud over Chuck's sector. We had the big one at last, and it was heading straight for the edge of the forest, the farm, One-One, and the rez.

Steve gave us an update: "All stations, this is Crescent Lake. Okay, guys, we've got the big one burning. We're pulling Fire Three back to a new line along fire lane three-seven-one, but we've made some progress on the west so we're going to be able to shift some assets. Stay with it."

The blowing smoke and ash made it impossible to sit long in one place. I went into the shack, washed my eyes, and then tied a wet bandanna across my nose and mouth like an outlaw in an old western. I circled the deck, watching for the twist of smoke from a spark-set fire in the hardwoods. I tried to picture Chuck and his crew fighting to establish the new line along 371. I'd been along the gravel fire lane more times than I could count, and I wondered what it looked like now as the bulldozers tore into the jack pines along its edges to widen the line and contain the fire. But nothing on earth was going to hold it back if it got into the crowns and started moving with the speed of the wind.

Noon came and went, but I didn't feel like eating. At one, Steve came on the air with another rundown of the news. The new line along 371 was holding, reinforced by men and equipment scraped together from other sectors. Volunteer fire departments from a dozen towns in the surrounding counties were on the way. The governor had called out the National Guard, and the Forest Service had three fire teams and two air tankers flying in from North Dakota.

Somebody keyed a mike: "Just a bit goddamn late from the look of things."

Steve snapped, "One-Six, I know your damned voice. Just can it and leave the comments for later."

The big one widened, overlapping the sectors north and south of Chuck's. At three, Steve keyed his mike, and we could hear voices shouting in the background. "All stations, we're going off the air for a while. The fire's breached the line south side sector two, and we've got to pull out. We'll be back up when we're mobile."

There was silence on the channel. Finally, Stella keyed her mike. "This is One-Seven. Understand you are evacuating. Is that an affirm, Over?"

"That's a roger, Godmother. We lost it, guys. We've got fire on the outbuilding roofs now."

"Jesus," somebody muttered.

"Just stay with it, guys. One-Seven, you are net

control. Air Spot is now on this channel. Fire Two is net control for fire-fighting."

"This is One-Seven, Roger. I am net control. Take care, Steve."

"Roger, this is Crescent Lake, Out."

Stella took the reports, her voice as calm as always, while the beautiful log buildings at Crescent Lake burned and Steve and the headquarters people ran for their lives. Forty-five minutes after he'd signed off, Steve came back on the air: "This is Crescent Lake mobile, I am net control. We are at Point Tango, one mile southwest of the lake. Call sign, Point Tango."

Stella adopted the new call sign as smoothly as if the change hadn't meant that a dozen buildings and God knows how many millions of dollars' worth of equipment hadn't just gone up in flames. "Roger, Point Tango. You are net control. We have new fires at . . ." She reeled off the list.

The spotting plane banked into the smoke, disappeared, and then came out of the cloud, its engine whining as it climbed. "Point Tango, this is Air Spot. We've got fire approaching three-seven-one north and south of Point X-ray. It looks mucho hot, moving fast."

"Roger, Air Spot. Take a look at smoke my bearing three-five-oh, range three miles."

"Roger, Point Tango. But we're going to have to make it fast. Those thunder boomers are coming in, and we'll have to get clear in ten. We'll refuel and get back up as soon as possible."

I watched as the thunderclouds rumbled in from the west, their bellies brushing the smoke, their lightning slashing at the pine. The radio crackled and popped, the transmissions breaking up as the towers called in strike after strike. The spinning gauge atop the shack whined as the treetops bent with the wind and the clouds rolled over the edge of the forest, heading straight for One-One. I closed the windows and sat in the hot seat. The world went dark and then exploded around me. I closed my eyes and prayed, to what I wasn't sure, as the tower groaned and shuddered. A deafening crack stunned me, and then rain sluiced down the windows, washing away the world beyond.

For ten minutes, it was like being inside a waterfall. Then the rain eased, the sky lightened, and I was still alive. I threw open the window, the breeze cool on my sweat-soaked shirt. I went out on the deck to watch the thunderclouds trundling east toward the rez. Below me the woods steamed. I circled the deck, looking for the telltale wisps of gray smoke in the mist. I found nothing, reached my chair, and sat, taking in lungfuls of the damp air.

The radio crackled. "All east side stations, this is Point Tango. Are you still with us?"

I reached through the window for the mike. "This is One-One. Still here." The other east side stations called in, some of the voices sounding scared. Over the forest, the rain had evaporated before it hit the ground and the smoke of the big

222

one rose as black as before. But the wind had eased and the column had straightened. I prayed again, wondered again if Chuck and his crew were still alive. Twenty minutes later, the wind was blowing harder than ever, the gauge atop the tower spinning at a steady thirty-five miles per hour, as the column of smoke tilted and lunged for the edge of the forest.

"All stations, this is Point Tango. We are moving again. Setting up Point Sierra, figures one-five minutes. One-Seven, you are net control."

Stella answered: "This is One-Seven, Roger. I am net control. Request status fire line at three-seven-one."

"It's breached. Crews falling back to fire lane three-seven-four."

"Roger, Point Tango."

I could hardly get my breath. Fire lane 374 was at the very edge of the forest, barely three miles away. If the fire broke through there, it would get into the dry hardwoods and open fields, where the wind would take hold and drive it at double the speed, crown fires sweeping ahead across the ribbons of pine splayed across the country between the forest and the rez.

The smoke and ash were almost unbearable outside, and I got ready to move into the shack. I made a final circuit of the deck to check for fires in the undergrowth. To my northeast, I caught a spot of rusty red amid the tossing branches of the birch and maple. I fixed my glasses in that direction and found it. For a long minute, I couldn't figure out what it was, and then I knew: a rusted red Dodge parked on an abandoned logging road that reached into the woods toward the muskeg swamp where the three tall pines sheltered the granite island.

I sat in the tower for another hour, forcing myself to concentrate on scanning the woods between One-One and the edge of the forest. It grew dark, the twilight coming fast under the blanket of smoke spreading over the country. One-Three called in, asked permission to leave the air, and got it. Ten minutes later, One-Four did the same. The radio crackled, Steve's voice tired and discouraged: "One-One, One-Two, One-Five, this is Point Sierra. You can hang it up, guys. Pull out while you've got the time." One-Five protested, and Steve made it an order. "No, we want you out now. Air Spot is back up, and we'll run him in to cover your territory. Good luck, guys. Thanks."

I acknowledged the order, switched off the radio, and went out on the deck to look a last time at the smoke, the fire, and the twilight. Then I shut the door of the shack and went through the trapdoor, climbing down the ladder to go looking for Jim as the tower shook and the stress cables thrummed in the wind blowing from the end of the world.

I found him a hundred yards from his car. He lay with his head resting against the spikes of an ancient hemlock log, his sightless eyes staring into the branches of the birch and maple tossing against the twilight sky. I touched his cold face, felt the congealed blood at the back of his skull where one of the spikes had entered, and then gathered him in my arms and pressed my face against his unbound hair and the dark streak of war paint on his cheek. He had come not as a drunken Chippewa boy poaching venison but as a warrior. And the dogwolf had killed him, hit him high in the chest, and driven him back against the spikes.

I don't know how long I held him, but at last I eased him down. His shotgun lay a half dozen feet from his outstretched right hand. I picked it up and ejected the spent shell, remembering the sound of what I'd thought was the backfire of a truck on the highway in the night. Jim had died out here before the fire had come to burn the world. If there was still time, maybe I could stop it, somehow break the chain by killing the dogwolf. I knelt by Jim, found a half dozen shells in his pocket, and reloaded the shotgun. My fingers were steady, a heat like boiling metal rising in my veins. I laid the gun down and reached behind his skull, felt the grittiness of dried blood and probed until my fingers came away wet. Slowly, I drew two fingers from my forehead, down my nose, to my chin. I tasted the iron-salt tang of his blood on my lips and knew that for at least this one night I, too, could go as a warrior into the dark. I stood, checked the shotgun once more, and stared into the twilight above the trees. *Entre chien et loup.*

*   *   *

I felt Jim walking beside me, knew that if I turned my head he would be there. Others followed in the shadows just beyond the corner of my vision where the branches of the trees glowed with a blue fire that did not burn. I knew them all: Harney and Wilson, a stern priest and a smiling young minister, an old medicine man using a crutch, a young hunter with his chest torn open by giant claws. And my father, striding supple and confident as a big bobcat, as we moved together toward the swamp where the dogwolf waited on the granite island in the shadow of three tall pines.

I crouched at the edge of the muskeg in the dark, knowing that they would not follow me across but would watch and wait in the shadow of the trees. The wind tore the clouds open, and a full moon broke through, riding high and cold in the roiling sparks and smoke. I stood, felt the shotgun heavy in my hands, and started across, my feet sinking into the moss, my shadow moving ahead of me across the muskeg by the glow of the fire and the light of the moon. At the island, I pulled off my boots and socks and slipped barefoot up the rock. Every few seconds, I waited for my breath to still and for the throb of my blood to recede until I could hear every rustle, every whisper beneath the wind. A pine snake slid down the granite, its scales burring on the stone as it wound past my leg and disappeared into a crevice at my feet. A scatter of frightened night swallows dipped into the pines and rose again, winging east away from the fire. I pulled myself forward, and like the snake, slid over the rock and into the bowl.

I stood, my bare feet on the granite and my back to the boulder where a hunter countless ages before had recorded a brother's death. A sudden down-draft whirled a cloud of smoke and sparks around me. It cleared and he was there, a dozen paces away, his eyes shining like he'd eaten the moon. For long heartbeats, we stared at each other. And then he let out a cry, half-whine half-howl, and came for me. I swung the shotgun up, already knowing that he was much too quick and that I would never have a second chance. The muzzle flash outlined the black shape of him, caught for an instant the dead-skull white of his teeth. He hit me chest high, sending the shotgun flying from my hands. My head smashed back against the boul-der, and the world snapped red, black, and red again. I fought to hold on to consciousness, fought to bury my fingers in his neck as I drove my teeth in at his jugular vein. I bit down, tasted fur and hide and a trickle of blood and knew that my human teeth couldn't tear his throat. My feet slipped on the granite and I fell, my head slamming into the rock and the blackness came rolling over me like a wave. The slab tilted under me, and I felt it sliding, felt it carrying the two of us back into the earth that had thrust it up a million years before. The dead weight of him held me down, pinned me to the granite, as his hot blood ran down my chest and over my stomach to grease our long slide down. The clouds rolled over, tumbled in on each other, and smothered the moon. The granite jerked, seemed to lift an inch, and then a crash as loud as all the thunder that ever was, ever could be, crushed the breath out of the night. The three tall pines exploded, lightning corkscrewing down their trunks like skyserpents racing straight for hell.

And then there was rain.

CHAPTER
TEN

I rolled the dogwolf off me and saw how the buck-shot from my single wild shot had shattered his chest. With my face turned upward into the steady rain, I leaned for a few minutes against the faded picture of the hunter killed by the bear. Then I crawled out of the bowl, found my boots, and stumbled across the muskeg by the light of the three burning pines.

It was raining steadily in the dawn when I guided Bert Weathers and another sheriff's deputy down the old logging road to where Jim's body lay half hidden in the ferns by the old hemlock log. Bert knelt, face grim, and I heard him murmur something in Chippewa. A prayer, a farewell? I did not know, because the words I might have known in the night were lost to me now. He reached out and gently closed Jim's staring eyes.

After they'd taken him away, I went back to the swamp and the granite island to find the dog-wolf. The three pines stood untouched by lightning or fire — as I'd known they would be — and the dogwolf, too, had come back into reality, a soggy black shape sprawled in the rocks where I'd left him. There was no need to hunt anymore, and I sat for a long time on a boulder in the rain with the dogwolf at my feet, trying to make sense of his story, of Jim's, and of my own. And when the rain had washed the blood from the dogwolf's coat and the tears from my cheeks, I dragged his body to a deep cleft between two boulders and walled him in forever.

It's been raining for a week now. Chuck and the fire teams stopped the big one at the last line, smashing it with bulldozers and bombing it with air tankers. The fire destroyed five thousand acres of timber, but the forest is big and the trees will grow again.

Mom, Chuck, and the girls are home now. Everyone is giving me room while I mourn for Jim. I haven't told them that I'm also grieving for the dogwolf — for what it was when it howled its rage and came for me in the rocks on the night I killed it. Perhaps Jim's talk of the shape-shifter came closest to the truth. The dogwolf was never quite one thing, never quite another. I think that even in Wilson's cage, it believed that it was a wolf trapped inside the body of a dog. But outside the cage, it could never quite make the shift and got caught in some terrible nowhere in between. So, I don't blame the dogwolf for trying to kill me that night; I gave it the freedom that drove it mad.

I guess I'm to blame for Jim's death and all the suffering that came of the dogwolf's madness. Yet there are things inside me that whisper other answers, that tell me that I was only a small part of what had to happen. Sometimes at night now, I go up on the ridge just to listen to the darkness. I think all the ghosts have gone — that Jim, Harney, old man Wilson, my dad, and the dogwolf have all slipped away, leaving me alone to make sense of what's left. Maybe there are some answers north of Fifty-Four beyond The Pas on the road to Flin Flon. Come autumn, I think I'll go find out.

About This Point Signature Author

ALDEN R. CARTER is an award-winning author of fiction and nonfiction for young adults. Among his novels are *Up Country*, *Sheila's Dying*, *Growing Season*, and *Wart, Son of Toad*, all ALA Best Books for Young Adults.

Mr. Carter lives in Marshfield, Wisconsin, with his wife, son, and daughter.